RUGOSA

CREEK STEWART

DROPSToNE PRESS
RUGOSA
Creek Stewart

Editor: Laura Markowitz
Copyeditor: Jacob Perry

Wholesale inquiries please visit http://www.dropstonepress.com

For more information about the RUGOSA book series, visit:
http://www.creekstewart.com

Published by DROPSToNE PRESS
ISBN 978-0-9976906-9-9

dropstonepress.com

ACKNOWLEDGMENTS

I would like to thank my amazing editor, Laura Markowitz, for believing in this project and for helping to bring my fabulous cast of characters to life.

DEDICATION

This book is dedicated to everyone who would risk everything to save the one person without whom they cannot survive.

CHAPTER ONE

The briar bushes and brambles rip at my clothes and face as I tear through the overgrowth beside the large open field of the valley. I hear shouting in a foreign language and then gunfire. My front fender explodes into pieces as a bullet tears through it. I lean forward into the bike and hear another round burst through my bug-out bag and hiss over my left shoulder. I feel liquid pouring down my back and panic for a minute thinking it's blood. It's too cold to be blood, I think. It's the water from my stainless steel bottle. But then I feel something hot and strange on my arm and my bike starts to slow down. A growing red stain catches my eye and I feel something warm running down my right arm. My hand is covered with blood and my grip on the accelerator is slipping. I quickly wipe the grip clean with the cuff of my shirt and wrench down on the accelerator again, lurching the bike forward.

It's unbelievable to me that just 24 hours ago I was relaxing in the meadow by the pond and enjoying freshly roasted frog legs and cattail heads.

– ONE DAY EARLIER –

Four years ago, I planted us a place to hide. Today, I walk deep into the woods to see how it's grown. The early morning light is just turning from gray to gold, and I move silently through the eastern West Virginia woods that I know like the back of my hand. I'm noting the places where rabbits have crossed the trail and where squirrels have buried their stash, even though I don't have time to lay any traps today. I take a deep breath of morning air and feel the familiar tingling in my chest—excited and alert. This woods is what I know. This is where I'm most alive.

I don't come visit here too often—don't want to break a trail, but it's been more than a year so I'm not too worried. I come over a hill covered with thin-trunked chinquapin oaks and the sight before me takes me by surprise: an impenetrable wall of thorns and brambles.

"This place will do," Grandpa had told me when I showed him this clearing four years ago. It's deep in the woods. Miles from anywhere. "But now you need a natural barrier that no one will question—something to keep them from looking too close." He considered it quietly for a moment, and then announced: "Rosa Rugosa. Plant yourself some Rosa Rugosa."

So I did. I carried ten small rose plants out here and put them in the ground, and now they've grown into a wild tangle. I can't see around it or through it, it's so thick.

"Grandpa, you were right," I say aloud, as if he were right beside me. "Exactly like you said. No one would think anyone could hide in the middle of this."

I chose this spot because the tree canopy is thin so it lets in a lot of sunlight, and there's a stream nearby that's fed by an underground spring. Rugosa grows new plants by sending out its roots. Those ten original plants have multiplied and grown together so densely that I'd need to be covered in kevlar to walk through it.

That's the point. It looks uninviting, which means it'll be a perfect spot for us to hole up when trouble comes.

When he'd lived in Nebraska, Grandpa told me, he'd planted rugosa around the perimeter of his barnyard to fence in the goats and chickens. I'd tried to imagine Mom's rose bushes as impassable fencing, but my imagination failed me. I'd never have guessed rugosa would have these razor-sharp thorns that look like mini eagle talons.

But as I move down the hill and get closer to the rugosa I see a problem. The tall shrubs are covered with crimson flowers that sparkle with dew. The flowers are eye-catching and they make this place memorable when I want people to just walk past and not really see it at all. I'll have to make sure I hide the entrance on the north side, where there aren't too many flowers. At least Macy will be happy. She loves roses, and when the flowers drop we can use the fruit—rose hips—for tea. It's a good source of Vitamin C.

That day he came here with me, Grandpa scratched out a plan in the dirt. "You plant the rugosa around the entrance to the bunker, and when the plants grow out you make a zigzag path through it, cutting low," he'd said. I was only 13 then, and I couldn't imagine what this place would look like in four years, so I nodded confidently and my Grandpa nodded back, like we had an understanding.

Now, I study the way the plant grows, with sharp spikes jutting out every which way, and I wonder if it can be cut without revealing the pathway in.

I walk around to the north side, where I'd made the opening to the bunker. Then I lie on my stomach against the leaf-littered ground and squint into the tangle of brambles. I let my mind relax. I imagine I'm a mouse scuttling away from an owl. Where would I dive into this thorny mess?

It's like one of those puzzles where you stare at all the wavy lines and suddenly you see the ducks on a pond. After a few minutes, I see it. I hop up, excited. I'll cut a few low brambles in the front that can be pulled aside to hide the opening, and then once the path is out of sight I can carve a low, wide path that we can belly-crawl through.

I reach for my machete. It hangs from my belt in a hand-made, cowhide sheath. That's when I feel that tight, choking feeling in my chest and I have to wait a minute for the feeling of grief to pass. Grandpa prepared me to do this. Maybe he knew he wouldn't be around when the time came. He even made me this machete. I remember watching him shape it from an old lawnmower blade, of all things. I'll take this over any of those cheap imports all day long. It's razor sharp, and tough, too. He made sure I knew how to sharpen it properly. While I honed it on his whetstone, he told me stories about Nebraska and summers on Boy Scout camporees with his friends. He told me about his grandfather, a member of the Omaha Nation, taking him out to hunt bear, and teaching him how to track and trap. As his hands deftly shaped the machete's wooden handle from a piece of 100-year-old oak with a file, Grandpa described the night that tree was struck by lightning, in the front yard of the family farm. He suddenly looked up from his carving and focused on me.

"Omaha, you remember: whoever uses this machete will have the steadiness of that old oak and the force of the lightning that took it down."

He knew I'd need both in the days to come. Those days are here, now. I only wish he was here with me.

***

It was a little more than two years ago when we got the news that Dad was dead. We hadn't heard from him in weeks, and I just knew in my gut that something had gone terribly wrong. Even after we were told, I felt a constant dread, a certainty that something else awful was going to happen. I told myself the worst had already come to pass losing Dad, but I was wrong. A year later, a group of international hackers struck the world's communications, banking, and transportation centers. They hit all the world's stock markets. The global economy crashed like a paper kite in a hurricane.

Then it was like dominoes. Other radical groups had been waiting for that first strike, and they poured oil on the fire. It was chaos in the cities. Mom kept the television on day and night until the power was shut down. What I saw still gives me nightmares. Half of the world's major cities turned to rubble or ruled by packs of roaming gangs.

Grandpa brought me up to be prepared. It's the Boy Scout motto. I'm third-generation Boy Scout. The machete in my hands reminds me of that fact. My fingers automatically trace the familiar letters on the oak handle that spell out my name: Omaha Hoyt. Grandpa burned it in with a hot poker from the makeshift forge he used to shape the blade. Below my name he drew our family symbol. It's a set of eagle wings, with the number 1 in the left wing and number 2 in the right wing. It stands for the 12 principles in the Scout Law: trustworthy, loyal, helpful, friendly, courteous, kind, obedient, cheerful, thrifty, brave, clean and reverent.

Grandpa liked to change brave to fearless when he recited it. He would say, "Omaha, remember that brave is for boys, and fearless is for men."

He and Dad each had our symbol tattooed on their right forearms. Grandpa started the tradition at age 17, when he earned the rank of Eagle Scout. He inked it himself with primitive tools handed down to him from his Omaha elders. He used the same tools to make my Dad's tattoo when he became an Eagle Scout at age 16, and he would have used them on me when I made Eagle. My Dad and Grandpa used to talk about how proud they were going to be when I got my tattoo. Grandpa called it the "Hoyt family crest."

Boy Scouts of America was outlawed six months ago, but I'll always be a Boy Scout. They can't take that away from me. I'm grateful every day that my Grandpa, Dad and my scoutmasters taught me what I need to know to survive out here in the woods.

I think about that as I crouch down by the boulder where I will start cutting the path into the rugosa snarl. It makes an easy marker for Mom and Macy, in case I'm not with them. "Fearless," I say, and swing the sharp blade.

Whack! The sound of the machete is out of place in these backwoods. The birds go quiet, but after a few more whacks they decide I'm not a threat and start up their chatter again. I cut carefully, following the path I scoped out. I warm to the work as I methodically chop a low way into the maze of thorns.

Grandpa warned me never to tell anyone except Mom about the bunker in the middle of the woods. I never questioned why we needed one. Even before the crash, we could all feel changes coming. It started with worldwide protests over international trade agreements, and then drones attacked the peaceful protesters around the world. It looked like a coordinated attack. Conspiracy theorists went nuts, and even skeptics started to wonder who was pulling the strings. Civil wars broke out in small countries in Africa and Central America, and some of the poorer Eastern European nations. Within a year, millions of refugees flooded Europe from Africa and the Middle East, and poured into the US through Mexico and Canada. More terrorist and extremist groups started bombing infrastructure. Half the railways in South America and Central America were disabled to protest corporations. Then came food shortages, water shortages, and pandemics in the refugee camps. Military collapsed and it was a free-for-all, with soldiers becoming mercenaries or forming up into gangs that terrorized their own people.

Countries ruled by dictators fared better because their people couldn't rise up, and those foreign governments saw an opportunity for expansion. They formed something called the World Union Government—the WUG. They called in our debt, and the world's debt. It was under this pretense that they took control of our communications and nuclear arsenal. All our news is controlled by the WUG now, so we don't really know what's happening out there, or who is in charge. We were told the Constitution has been "temporarily suspended" and we are now subjects of the WUG.

The United States is no longer a superpower. The invaders are still consolidating their hold, though. Their troops on the ground on the East and West Coasts are rumored to be quelling the uprisings and bringing back order and peace, but Mom says if you listen between the lines of their news broadcasts, which are blatant propaganda, it's clear they're just here to steal what they can and make us work for them. They're distracted by the rich cities now, but it won't be long until the WUG turns its attention to plundering the countryside. We still have plenty of coal and natural gas here in this part of West Virginia. The WUG will be coming, there's no doubt about it. There isn't much time to get ready for the invasion that's heading our way.

***

Grandpa never recovered from the news about Dad. He grieved in silence, but tears ran down his cheeks as he carved the Hoyt family crest on the grave marker. We placed the marker up on the hill behind the house, even though there was no body to bury. Dad died far from home. We were not allowed to know where. Maybe that's what broke Grandpa's heart—not being able to see his only son one last time or to know if his death was peaceful.

Grandpa passed just a few months later. I found him lying in the field back behind the barn. Mom said his heart just gave out. I cried as I dug his grave up on the hill beside Mom's roses and next to Dad. I chiseled the Hoyt family crest on Grandpa's gravestone. I tried to make it look exactly like the one he'd made for Dad. I added the words "Brave and fearless" on the bottom. Grandpa and Dad both were both brave and fearless, but I'm not. I'm not a lot of things listed in the Scout Law.

I worry all the time about how I'm going to keep Mom and Macy safe. I worry all the time about whether I've lost London.

It's hard to think about her without getting a sick feeling in my gut. I have no choice but to live with it and move on, I guess, but I still miss her like she left yesterday. Is that normal?

London moved to Philadelphia a few weeks after we buried Grandpa. We were both fifteen that spring, but London always seemed a lot older than me. She and her dad had moved into the house down the road when we were seven. Her mom had died of cancer the year before. London's dad didn't know what to do with his only child. He had to leave her at home alone for weeks at a time while he drove around the state selling auto parts. London said he was never quite right after her mom died, but I'm sure the alcohol didn't help either. When Mom found out London was all alone, she made up a bed in Macy's room and then walked over to London's house, packed up her things and brought her over to live with us. I didn't hear what she said to London's dad when he finally came back home to check on his daughter, but he agreed to sign papers giving Mom and Dad legal guardianship. I was happy to give London my room once it was clear. She was an official part of the family. I moved up to the attic.

From the first day we met, London was my best friend. She's the only person outside my family who I can be myself around. Before London, I kept to myself and avoided other kids. School was just something to get through. But once London showed up, school was an adventure because she was there. London was like a sun breaking through dark clouds, shining unexpected light and warmth on people. When she made up daring games at recess, everyone wanted to play with us. She could even charm our teachers into having class outside when the weather was nice. London immediately became the most popular kid in our class, and as her best friend I started to get noticed more and the other kids invited me to go along with them, even though I never liked to say much. The best times were when it was just London and I exploring together in the woods. She is the most amazing, magical person I've ever met. She's smarter, faster and more confident than me, but I never cared about that. I just loved to be around her, to hear her laugh and tease while we climbed trees and waded in streams.

London was jealous of me regarding one thing: Boy Scouts. When we were seven, Mom offered to sign her up for Girl Scouts, but London insisted that only Boy Scouts would do. Grandpa didn't say anything, but when it was time to drive me over to our Scoutmaster's house for our troop meeting, he nodded to London and she jumped in the car. She came to nearly every meeting after that, and Grandpa brought her along on our camping trips, too, setting her up her own tent next to his. She was better at most everything than all the boys in our troop, but no one minded, because she was London. When we were ten, her knife skills were better than the Scoutmaster's, so he put her in charge of teaching all the new scouts knife safety. We never had any knife accidents in our troop after that.

About me, Mom used to always say, "Omaha's not shy; he's a loner." Now I wonder about that. Can you be a loner if you're always missing someone? If you're always having conversations in your mind with her?

London used to get teased because of her name, but I think it fits her. She was always out of place here in eastern West Virginia, like something bright and shiny surrounded by dull, gray gravel. In high school, the most popular guys asked her out on dates to the movies and school dances. Sometimes she went, and those nights I stayed home and felt sorry for myself and watched the clock, wondering when she'd get home. I hated sharing her, but I never told her how I felt. I kept my feelings hidden as best I could.

The day she left was the third saddest day of my life. Mom tried to console me, saying, "London has a restless spirit." But the truth was that I wasn't enough for her after Grandpa died. It's a bitter truth. I wasn't enough of a reason for her to stay.

She wouldn't have left if Grandpa hadn't died. They had a

special bond. He took her out hunting, and though she never was a big fan of the killing part, she loved to work with the furs, hides and feathers. He called her "the best Eagle Scout I ever knew." One day, when I was nine, she found me trying to sew a merit badge on my sash. She took it from my clumsy hands and put in a row of perfect stitches. After that, Grandpa set her up with some simple leatherwork and she made a pouch. It was so cleverly designed that it could fold up flat and then open up with four small inner compartments. Even Grandpa couldn't have made something like that! He told her she was a natural. Mom gave her a hug and said this was probably what it was like when Mozart played his first piano. London had a gift for leatherwork.

Grandpa set her up with her own workbench in the saddle shop and she'd sit in there for hours sewing and molding her own creations while I hung around by the door whittling, or tying fishing flies with Grandpa. By the time she was thirteen, London had regular customers around the world thanks to Internet sales. She was even commissioned to make a leather arrow quiver for a Hollywood movie. All that money went into the special savings account Mom had started for her, along with the occasional checks London's father sent for Christmas (and, when he remembered, her birthday). London never wanted to spend a dime of it. I didn't really think much about what she might have been saving up for.

London made me a few small things over the years. A braided wristband that fell off and washed away while we were swimming in the quarry. A wallet, which is so nice I never take it anywhere because I don't want to lose it. She also made my cowhide machete sheath. That was a present for my fourteenth birthday. On the day she left she gave me one last present. I was

angry and hurt. I didn't want anything from her. I just wanted
her not to leave me, but I accepted the wooden box from her
hands.

"Omaha," she said. (I loved hearing her say my name.) "I
made these moccasins for you. I made them for when you go
hunting. I used three layers of emu hide for the soles so that
you can feel everything on the forest floor. Emu is very thin, but
really tough and almost impossible to puncture. The uppers are
a combination of raccoon, possum, coyote and the insides are
lined with fox fur to keep your feet warm on really cold days.
The laces are made from that elk you and Grandpa took last fall.
There's a little bit of all of us in these moccasins."

I replay this scene over and over in my head and I wish I'd
opened my mouth and told her what I was feeling. I'm not
good with words, and I guess I also knew nothing I could say
would have changed her mind. But at least I'd know she knew
how I felt.

The way I rewrite that moment in my head, I say to her, "I
can go with you," and she smiles and nods and we get on my
dirt bike and drive off together. I wanted to go with her, but I
wasn't invited. And London knew that I couldn't leave Mom
and Macy. She also knew that I don't like big cities. I don't
like noise and the crowds. I am never able to feel comfortable
around lots of people. I haven't even been to the town of
Manchester, which is only 14 miles away, since we saw London
board the bus there. I stayed out in the woods for days after,
roaming around aimlessly and feeling her absence everywhere
I went. I thought our life was perfect here. We have everything
we need. Why would London choose to go live in Philadelphia?
It has no meadow, no garden with Mom's special purple
tomatoes, no forest where you can walk for days and not meet

another soul. And no me.

But London was undeniably eager to go the day she grabbed her big, hand-made leather duffel bag and got on that bus. She was smiling and laughing more than usual at breakfast, joking with Macy and giving Mom big hugs. Mom had worked it out that London would spend the summer with Grandpa's younger sister, Miki, who owned a small tailoring shop in South Philly. Miki was getting really old and needed help. London told me that someday she was going to open her own boutique store and call it London Leather.

"Miki will teach you how to run a business," Mom said sagely. It's true, but I was mad at Mom for helping London leave us.

I'm not proud of how I acted that day. I moped around and sulked. Mom pulled me aside before we left for town to see her off.

"London doesn't show it, but she's taking Grandpa's death hard. He was like a father to her, you know." I did know that. "It will be good for her to get away and see some new sights, and you can stand to be apart from her for a few weeks. It'll just be for the summer. She'll be back in no time."

"No time" turned into two years and counting. Not a day goes by when I don't wish she were here. I miss Dad and Grandpa, sure, but they couldn't come back even if they wanted to. But London – she could. She doesn't want to. That thought forms a hard knot in my gut. Every morning when I wake up I expect to hear her laughing in the kitchen with Macy. I start to call out to her to hurry up and meet me in the meadow so we can check the traps. I've nearly worn out the few pictures I have of her, and I don't think those photographs do my memories justice anyway.

London did plan on staying only for the summer, but then Miki died and in her will she'd left her tailoring shop to London. Mom sent London all that money she'd saved up and London invested it in a website and upgrades to Miki's store. She also sent a picture of the big brown sign she'd made for her store. It said "London Leather" and it was made of leather. At 15, she'd realized her dream. I should have been happy for her, but I wasn't. To me it meant I lost her for good.

London used to call Mom every Sunday, before the crash. I'd hang around the kitchen and pretend not to be listening to Mom's end of the conversation, and then Macy's enthusiastic chatter. Macy would offer the phone to me and I'd usually shake my head. Mom made me talk to her once, and as I knew it would be, it was awkward. I'm not much for the telephone. The next week, there was a letter for me in the mail. She knew I didn't like the Internet, either. I stared at her messy handwriting, so different from the neat little stitches she can make in leather. Anyway, it was a newsy letter telling me about the store and the commissions she'd gotten. She signed it "Love and Leather, London," and then added a P.S. "Come visit!" It felt like something someone says to be nice. I told myself if she'd meant it she wouldn't have stuck it on at the end like it was an afterthought. I took it as a sign that she doesn't care about me the way I care about her.

To be honest, I might have gone anyway, but I get filled with dread at the thought of navigating a big city and all those strangers in it. I wrote back and added a P.S. of my own. "Wish I could visit, but I have to look after things here." I suppose we were both stubborn, and it certainly didn't help my aching heart to stay away from her, but I knew I'd hate seeing her life in Philadelphia. Everything would be different between us. We

wouldn't be able to walk in the meadow at twilight and catch
fireflies, or wade up the creek to collect cattails to roast for a
picnic the way we used to do every summer growing up. I feel
a stir of excitement when one of her letters comes, but I also get
a sick feeling in my stomach when I read about all the friends
she's made. She doesn't mention any by name and I wonder if
she has a boyfriend. I wonder if she's keeping it from me on
purpose because she feels sorry for me. That bothers me.

I know London loves me, but I must accept that it's not the
same kind of love I have for her. Or maybe my love has changed
since she's been gone. I'm 17 now, not a boy anymore. I love
her like a man loves a woman, but I suspect she loves me like a
sister loves a brother.

***

Now there's no chance I can visit her. She might not ever
be able to come home. That thought chills me. In the two
years since she moved away, the whole world has changed. The
WUG is based somewhere in Eurasia. They try to make it seem
like they're the new United Nations, but that's a joke. We're
now owned by the countries we owed money to for years. Our
national debt was sky-high and economists all agreed that there
was no way we would ever pay it back, not in 20 generations.
The president and other politicians told us that joining the
WUG would be a good thing because we wouldn't owe money
anymore. Only the most ignorant people believed that. The
rest of us knew we were being sold out, but there was nothing
we could do about it. We had no more money to pay for the
upkeep of our nukes, our power plants or our military. If the
WUG countries wanted, they could have rolled right over all
fifty states and blasted us to pieces with our own drones and
bombers. Mom said there were a lot of countries that probably

wanted to see the United States get leveled with bombs. I guess we've made some enemies during our decades as a superpower. But the WUG decided it was more profitable to move in and help themselves to whatever they want.

Some people still try to convince themselves that the WUG is a good thing. I heard some guy on the radio argue that the United States might come back one day, humbled, but better than before. Our school principal mumbled something like this in our last general assembly before announcing that the schools were all being temporarily shut down by order of the WUG until they could draw up a new national budget and see if education was "fundable in the new economic reality." Any schooling is done at home now, like Mom does with Macy and a few neighbor kids.

The day WUG representatives met with the President in Washington, they signed an order together dissolving Congress and the Supreme Court and nullifying the Constitution in favor of the WUG martial laws. The President ordered the U.S. armed forces to disband peacefully and surrender all weapons to the WUG. He gave the nuclear codes and locations of the silos to the WUG chairman, whose name we are not allowed to know. The last order President Morhead signed was his own resignation, and then the Executive branch was dissolved.

Even people who didn't know what the Constitution said missed it when we didn't have it anymore. The press was shut down. It became illegal for more than four unrelated people to gather in one place at any given time. Guns were outlawed. Free speech was outlawed. The right to a fair trial was outlawed. We are forced to live under martial law. Owning a representation of the U.S. flag is now against the law. We're not the United States of America anymore. The WUG renamed us Unimerica. They set up a new capitol somewhere in Canada, I heard, but orders come from WUG headquarters in Eurasia.

The other thing that changed is our money. Overnight, the US Dollar became worthless. Everything bought and sold, including food, medicine, and fuel is controlled and tracked by UNIM, the WUG division that monitors all Unimericans and issues UNIM Identification Cards. All Unimerican citizens are required to have one. Cash is worthless. The banks are all gone; Fort Knox was cleaned out. There are no more credit cards. In the first week, the WUG started leasing our land to multinational corporations. They're tearing up forests and knocking down mountains to dig out the copper, coal, natural gas, petroleum and other minerals, and creating mega-farms that use toxic chemicals and genetically modified crops. That food is shipped back to Eurasia. I've heard Yellowstone National Park has been completely stripped to bare earth for mineral resources and Mount Rushmore has been ground to gravel to build mining roads in and out of the west.

When the food shortages started up in the cities, WUG soldiers marched in and shot the front line of demonstrators and then rounded up the rest and threw them into work camps. That's the labor they use for the mines and mega-farms. The smallest offense against the WUG is punishable by a 10-year work-camp sentence. Whatever you call them, those camps are nothing but a glorified form of slavery. Our neighbor got sent there just because she complained when a local WUG official in Manchester cut to the front of the line at the gas station.

What I hate most is how they reward snitches. You can earn extra food and fuel credits by reporting anti-WUG behavior, which is basically what any WUG official deems unpatriotic to Unimerica. London managed to get a letter through to us a few months ago that said some people in Philadelphia make their entire living by turning their neighbors and family members in. Knowing this only reinforces my natural tendency to dislike people.

After our military was disbanded, including the National Guard, the WUG let police personnel know that they could enforce the new laws or be sent to concentration camps called UNIcation Centers. We heard that more than half were shot by firing squads. The survivors were farmed out to the work camps to be guards and enforcers. In the meantime, millions of troops from WUG countries were deployed to Unimerica to put down all the revolts that have been springing up in the big cities – or so we've been told by WUG-controlled television. It's hard to know what's true anymore. They monitor what's left of the Internet so even that's not a reliable source of information.

Every day it seems like there's more bad news. Countless bans have been established, outlawing almost everything that made the United States of America so great. It is now considered illegal to own any kind of lethal weapon; to travel more than 100 miles without a WUG-issued travel permit; to stockpile food or medicine; to grow a garden, raise livestock, hunt and gather from the wild; and to exceed the daily quotas for fuel consumption, water and electricity usage, Internet bandwidth and grocery supplies. Schools are closed. Civic groups are outlawed. We no longer have the right to peaceful assembly. No Boy Scouts. Churches are boarded up. More than four non-family members gathered in one place is illegal. There is no justice system, no trial or jury. If you're caught doing something illegal, or if you're even suspected of an infraction, any WUG official can sentence you on the spot to severe work-camp sentences. We've heard of plenty of people who were sent to the camps. No word has yet come back from any of them, so we don't really know what goes on there, but it can't be good.

We stopped holding Boy Scout meetings many months ago. The Boy Scouts of America has been disbanded completely and wearing the uniforms is considered an act of WUG treason. The Boy Scouts stood for everything the WUG hated about America. Someone from my troop overheard WUG soldiers in Manchester say that as long as people saw scouts in uniform they would still have hope for a brighter tomorrow. I broke the law that week by not letting the WUG confiscate my uniform. I have Dad's and Grandpa's too, in fact. I hid them in the bunker along with our Boy Scout Manuals and patches. The WUG soldiers were right; they do represent hope, and I can't stand by and let a bunch of foreign invaders laugh as they burn them in the town square with all the United States flags, which have also been confiscated. (I've got one of those in the bunker, too!)

Mom, Macy and I had a serious discussion last week and we agreed we will not register with UNIM to get identification cards, but we are also aware that this decision will eventually catch up with us one way or another. The UNIM Identification Card allows you to get food, fuel, medicine and clothes from the WUG-controlled supply, but the price for all Unimerica Citizens is that the WUG can keep track of you. They know what you're buying, where you live and where you go. What's worse is that they've started rounding up people with UNIM cards and sending them to UNIM Participation camps, which are basically work camps that are supposed to be a little nicer than the regular work camps. No one I know has ever been to one and come back, so I can't say what it's like. In my opinion, all the WUG camps are prisons, no matter what they call them.

I lay awake at night worrying about London. We've heard

stories of ghost towns that sprung up overnight when WUG soldiers rounded up all the people in a town or suburb and took them all away in armored trucks, even the babies and old people. London got a letter to us through an underground smuggling network. She wanted us to know she was safe, and not to worry, but she said it was true that Bryn Mawr, a suburb of Philly, turned into a ghost town overnight. She said everyone in the city was in a panic about it.

Are Mom, Macy and I making the right decision not to register with the UNIM? When you're prey, staying off the predator's radar is the first rule of survival. But we're on our own now. If something should happen to me, will Mom and Macy survive? We don't have any back-up. It's just us. Even though we're doing pretty well on our own, I worry about all the what-ifs. What if I get hurt? What if Mom needs medical attention? Can we really pull this off?

Those are my night worries. During the day, I feel centered. I know what to do. I feel more at home in the woods than in our house and we've got good food on the table. I try not to stay out in the woods for more than a few days at a time, tracking, stalking and hunting wild game. I don't want to leave Macy and Mom alone for too long. We're lucky to live out in the country where there is abundance of food, as long as you know where to look for it.

Also, during the day, I remember that we have neighbors we can go to if we need help. They feel the same about the WUG. Mom quietly barters with an underground network, getting us supplies that we can't make, catch, kill, grow or find on our own. My old Cub Scout den leader, Mr. Hammond, runs a real nice barter business by trading honey he harvests from camouflaged bee hives hidden in secret places. He's shown me a few of them and they are almost impossible to detect. (The WUG outlawed all food production. They want us to be fully dependent on them.) I also know of several operational liquor stills located in the woods. I've never stuck around long enough to see who runs them, but they're hidden extremely well. I notice everything that's out of place in the woods, but I doubt the average person would see them. One I've seen is disguised as a tall, hollow tree, and another is dressed as a round hay bale at the edge of a large hay field.

But bartering is not going to be enough. One day, the WUG will come after those of us who haven't joined UNIM. When they do, we'll need a place to hide. I'm grateful Grandpa had me build the secret bunker and plant the rugosa. We can hide in plain sight, like the beehives.

***

There are whispers on the subnet of a well-organized group of revolutionaries in the cities who are planning a revolt to end WUG rule, but I think it's just wishful rumors. Anyway, I have enough to think about without getting involved in all that. I'm focused on keeping me, Mom, Macy and London (if she would ever come home) fed, safe and alive. Last night, I went with Mom to a barter meet in a neighbor's barn. I heard talk about a rebel group that wants to organize us country people into a secret militia. I listened, but I wasn't convinced. Anyone can see it's not a battle we can win. The WUG has drone bombers; we have slingshots.

We were supposed to surrender our guns when the WUG took over, but Mom, Macy and I kept our hunting rifles and shotguns. We don't use them much because ammunition is scarce, but I feel safer knowing we have them in case of an emergency. I use bow and arrow for hunting. In the meantime,

I'm glad I was already adept at the primitive hunting techniques Grandpa taught me when I was younger. Many people who held out for the first year ended up joining UNIM in the end because they just couldn't get enough meat without their hunting guns. Between the garden Mom and Macy tend, and their canning, and my hunting and trapping, we've been able to meet our own needs, build a small amount of food storage, and have some left over to barter for our other necessities. I've even been able to mail London an occasional food package through the smuggler's network. I always include a letter to let her know exactly what's going on back at home, but I write it in somewhat of a code, because the WUG might intercept it. I want London to know what's happening here, and that she has a safe place here if she can make it back. This will always be her home, too. I need her to remember that.

My last letter talked about how fast Macy is growing up – she is 14 now – and how I expanded the garden this spring and also used part of the meadow to plant wheat and barley. I told her how big the rugosa patch is getting. London thought I was crazy when I finally spilled the secret. I know Grandpa said only to tell Mom, but I've never been able to keep a secret from London. I made a coded reference to it in my letter. I also described how pretty the apple blossoms are in the orchard this year and even included a dried one that I pressed in a book on my desk. And, as I always do, I told her how we all miss her here at home. It's just not the same without her, especially for me.

We heard from her once more since that letter. The message came last night. A different courier slunk into the barter meet just as we were ending. I didn't like the looks of him. His eyes were shifty, but maybe he was just nervous. We all were.

He asked around and then came over to Mom and showed her the letter. She paid him with deer jerky and a jar of apple butter. His eyes went wide. WUG rations are mostly tasteless, processed protein.

We saved the letter until we got home, and then read it by candlelight. London writes that she's been able to make ends meet in Philadelphia by converting Miki's shop into a repair and tailor shop that caters to the WUG military personnel. She's the go-to seamstress in that area for all alterations and gear repair for hundreds of soldiers and WUG officials. No one can be successful under the current circumstances unless they somehow cooperate with the WUG. I know her pride keeps her rooted in Philadelphia, but I have a bad feeling about London doing business with the enemy. I wish she would come home before things get worse.

This is what's on my mind as I take most of the morning to carve a path through the Rosa Rugosa bushes. I weave in and out of the bushes very carefully to create a path that doesn't appear to be a path. By the time I finish I've got quite a few scratches on my hands, but nothing too deep.

I decide to break for lunch before heading back home to help Mom and Macy finish planting the potatoes. I grab a handful of dried, fluffy seedpods at the wood's edge and have a small fire going in no time with the help of the fire striker I keep on a leather thong around my neck. After piling on a few larger sticks to create a good, hot, coal bed, I head for the pond just over the hill. On my way I cut down a small willow sapling with my machete. It's about one inch in diameter and eight feet long. I quickly trim off the branches and split the bottom into four equal sections about ten inches up. I press a small rock to the bottom of the splits, which spreads the four sections apart. I then carve the four sections to sharp points. This creates a very effective split-tip frog gig.

"Watch out, frogs," I think to myself as I creep silently behind a stand of cattails. In a few minutes I have speared four large bullfrogs, which gives me eight nice-sized legs for lunch. As I dress and clean them on a big rock next to the pond, I pretend to explain to a small pine tree how it's done.

"You see, Mr. Pine, you slice a belt around their waist and just pull off their pants. It's as easy as that!"

No one is around to hear me, so I don't feel embarrassed that I'm talking to a tree.

Before I head back to the hot coals I decide to use the head and entrails from one of the frogs and set a bank line using a hook and length of twine from my fishing kit, which I always keep in my backpack. Be prepared!

"Maybe you will get dinner for me," I say to the tree, while tying off the tail end of the bank line to the trunk of Mr. Pine. "I'll be back tonight to see, and hopefully you won't disappoint me."

On my way back to the fire I snap off a few green seed heads from the cattails to roast with my frog legs.

"Just like mini ears of corn," I remember Grandpa saying with a chuckle. He always had a taste for cattail heads.

I'm full after two cattail-on-the-cob and four frog legs, so I wrap the other four legs and cattail cobs in a great burdock leaf and head for home.

It is early afternoon by the time I get there and Mom and Macy are still in the garden.

"You guys hungry?" I unfold the burdock leaf and offer the snack on the wheelbarrow.

"Frog legs!" Macy's freckled face splits into a big grin. "My favorite! Can Tunnel have one?"

Tunnel is Macy's pet fox and loyal companion. Mom smiles at me and then at Macy and gives a nod. Macy looks just like Mom, with curly brown hair pulled back into a thick braid, thoughtful brown eyes, and sure hands that can knit, weave, sew, plant and shuck peas so fast they are almost a blur. Since school closed, they spend all day, every day, together. They're as close as best friends. With a pang, I miss my best friend, who is far away in the city, and Dad and Grandpa, who are never coming home. But I'm glad Mom and Macy have each other.

As I watch Macy play with Tunnel I can't help but remember a conversation I had with Mom just after London left, before we'd ever heard of the WUG. We were on the edge of the meadow picking raspberries in July.

"Omaha," she said, "do you remember when you guys brought Tunnel home from the woods?"

"Like it was yesterday."

"Remember how Tunnel loved playing inside with Macy?"

"Yes," I said with a smile. "I remember how she destroyed all of my dried elk jerky, too." I wondered what this had to do with anything.

"But over time she changed. Tunnel seemed depressed and not herself," Mom continued. "Being inside wasn't enough for her and she yearned for the woods. What did Macy have to do?"

"She let Tunnel go back to the wild," I answered, remembering Macy's tear-stained face as she let the beloved fox go and Tunnel ran off into the woods.

"And then what happened?"

"Tunnel came back a few weeks later." I saw where Mom was going with this.

"That's right," Mom said. "Tunnel came back. Tunnel made that choice. But more importantly, Macy let her make that choice. That wasn't easy for Macy." Mom placed her hand on my shoulder and stared directly in my eyes. "It's the same way with London, Omaha. We have to let her go and hope she comes back. She has to experience the world to know that this is where she wants to be."

"Why can't she just know it?!" I'd said, banging my raspberry pail down on a rock in frustration.

Mom ignored my outburst. "The problem is that you want London to need you. But you shouldn't want her to need you. She can take care of herself. What you should want is for her to want you. But London needs to see the world in order to know what she really wants."

Mom was right, of course (annoyingly). But how could I make London want me? "Do you think she'll come back, Mom?" I was trying to hold back my tears.

"I don't know, sweetheart," she replied softly. "I sure hope so, but she's struggling with a lot of emotions right now. Her mom died when she was just a girl. Her dad abandoned her and now Grandpa has died. On an emotional level, needing people scares her, because they leave her. She's confused. She needs some time to sort things out."

Tunnel's high-pitched yipping for more frog legs jolts me back to the present.

"I don't have any more, Tunnel," I say while scratching between her ears. "You ate them all."

"Omaha, you got a letter from London today," blurts Macy with her mouth full.

"It's in the kitchen," Mom adds, knowing that I'll be anxious to read it. "Neighbor brought it by. It was in a package the courier brought him last night, with a leather wristband in payment for bringing it over."

My heart races. Why didn't London send it directly to us? I sense danger.

"We read our part, but left yours in the envelope," Macy says. London always writes three separate letters – one to each of us.

I hear them whispering as I jog to the house. I like to sit at Dad's desk when I read letters from London. I don't know why, because I never sit there for any other reason. Maybe it's because I'm always bracing myself for bad news and I hope some of Dad's fearlessness will rub off on me if I sit in his chair. I'll admit it: I get nervous every time I open a letter from her.

Dear Omaha,

I hope you and Mom and Macy are doing well. Thank you so much for the food package last week. Your wild turkey jerky is my favorite and Mom's bread mix is the best I've ever had. I've been selling the hides you send. The WUG soldiers pay a lot. I kept the fox fur you sent, though. I think it's the prettiest I've ever seen.

Philadelphia is getting worse. The uprisings are taking a toll on this old city and the WUG are getting nastier. Rebels vandalized my shop last week because I tailor WUG uniforms. I'm just lucky I wasn't working late or I might have been in the shop when they came. They smashed out all the windows and made a mess of all my tools and materials.

I feel trapped between two worlds – the rebels on one side and the WUG on the other. Being in the middle is getting more and more dangerous.

Maybe it's time for me to come home. I miss you, Mom and Macy and the pond and meadow. There is a WUG caravan

heading west the week after next. I am going to trade my WUG
credits to get a travel permit and catch a lift on it. I'll see you soon.
Fingers crossed.
  Love & Leather,
  London

My heart literally stops. I re-read the letter three times to
make sure I'm not just seeing things.

"She's coming back," I mutter out loud.

"She's coming back!" I scream, running out the door to the
garden. "She's coming back!!!"

Mom and Macy are almost as excited as I am. We all three
hug and dance around, laughing deliriously. That knot that's
been in my chest for the past two years is melting away. I
haven't felt this happy since before Dad died.

"Omaha, this calls for a celebration," Mom says with
excitement in her voice. "Why don't you go down to the pond
and get one of the yearling ducks, and we'll have roast duck for
dinner tonight. It's about time we had some good news around
here."

Dinner is absolutely delicious. It's not often that we treat
ourselves to a feast. Roast duck with fresh wapato tubers that
I gathered from the pond and last fall's apples from the root
cellar, which Mom fries in butter. Macy makes a wild mint tea
sweetened with honey that I traded a batch of fresh-water river
mussels for with my old scoutmaster. And for dessert we split
a big piece of sweet fig flatbread soaked in warm milk. At this
moment, I'm happy and full and can't stop grinning because
London is coming home! Macy talks happily about the feast
we'll make when London gets home, and she and Mom start
planning how they will fix up London's room tomorrow. None

of us have touched it since she left, but Mom made a full coyote fur quilt for her bed. I know she'll love it.

After dinner, we turn on the evening news. We are just in time to catch the announcement that another great American city has been "saved from rebel chaos by the heroic WUG." I don't know who they think they are fooling with their propaganda. A scrolling announcement on the television screen reads:

The World Union Government has taken efforts to protect its Unimerican Citizens living around the city by quarantining and containing dangerous rebel outbreaks and revolts. Lawlessness will not be tolerated.

Mom and I shoot each other a look of alarm. If too many citizens start to rebel in the big cities, the WUG's response is to quarantine the city and block all major routes in and out with foreign military troops. No transportation of goods or services enters or leaves the city. They disable all utilities including water, electricity, waste removal and gas. Then they just let the city destroy itself from the inside out. After a few days of rioting and chaos, they finish it off with a few large-scale destroyer bombs. The WUG press covers it in detail to make sure the world sees the price of rebellion.

All the good feelings we just had drain away. Mom, Macy and I watch in silence as the black and white text announcement transitions to live footage of the city riots. The smoke from fires and screams from people stuck in buildings are too much for Macy, who hides her face in her hands. I want to do the same, but somehow I can't look away.

"The city has been shut down since 2 p.m. today,"

announces the reporter. "As you can see by the military barricades behind me on I-95, no one is allowed in or out of the city."

The camera angle switches to a WUG armed vehicle dragging what looks like a huge bell through the downtown streets.

"Is that the Liberty Bell?" gasps Mom.

The WUG has a habit of destroying national landmarks, so it wouldn't surprise me if it were.

Then it hits me. "Philadelphia. Oh my God, the Liberty Bell is in Philadelphia!"

My entire life changes in one split second.

"Omaha, you can't go!"

CHAPTER TWO

Macy is lying on my bed, tears streaming down her face. She's clasping my pillow in her arms as if it wants to leave her, too.

"I have to go, and you know it," I quietly respond as I pull my scout pack from under my bed. I'll need a larger pack than the small one I carry every day in the woods. Mom is standing by the door to my room, watching me pack. "Mom, you know I can't let her die in that city, and that's what will happen if I don't get there fast. She only has a few days before they send in the drone bombers." I don't say what we're all thinking: London might already be dead. Mom doesn't argue, but her face is tight and worried. I stop packing to hug her.

"I love you and Macy, but I have to leave as soon as I can. Dad would've gone to get you, and I'm going to get her."

Her shoulders slump and I can tell she understands and she's not going to try to talk me out of it. Mom loves London like a daughter. And she knows I'm right about Dad.

Dad worked on contract for the military before the United States joined the WUG. He wasn't a soldier, exactly. They hired him as a specialist in the art of stalking and tracking. He spent the last few years before his death helping special ops teams track the Gi-Nong warriors through the jungles of South Asia. He'd come home for a few months at a time and then they'd send him back over there. When he was home, he spent all of his time training Macy and me in survival skills to prepare us for what he called the "tougher times ahead." I guess it didn't take a genius to see that the country was heading for hard times, but I doubt even he imagined times as tough as these, and certainly not the journey that awaits me now.

I'm going to need all the skills he and Grandpa taught me to get to Philadelphia, get London, and bring us both home safely. They taught me how to stalk and hunt wild game and how to be invisible in plain sight. They taught me how to identify and harvest wild plant edibles in every season and how to build makeshift survival shelters in virtually any weather condition. Grandpa showed me how to improvise primitive weapons for hunting and self-defense, and also how to weave cordage from certain trees and plants. Dad made sure I was skilled in a variety of improvised small-game traps. It occurs to me now that he always pointed out how most of the snares we used could also be sized up to catch large game – and adult men, if necessary. He'd even shown me some of the traps the Gi-Nong used against U.S. soldiers in the jungle. Even though Dad was hired to track the Gi-Nong, the way he spoke of them suggested a certain level of mutual respect. Truth be told, I think he identified more with the Gi-Nong rebels than with the US soldiers who hunted them. I don't know much about the Gi-Nong except that they were native to the jungles and resented U.S. companies coming in and mining their mountains for ore and drilling for oil and logging their timber.

I frantically throw items I'll be taking with me onto the bed. My mind is racing as I try to imagine what kinds of weather and conditions I'll be facing between here and Philadelphia.

"Son," Mom says, "you need to slow down and think. Your father and grandfather would have never prepared for a hunt like this. You don't even know what you're marching into. You have to think this through."

"She's right, Omaha," chimes Macy. "I know you want to get out of here as fast as possible, but you have to make sure you have everything you need."

"She could be dying right now!" I never scream at Mom and Macy and immediately I regret it. "I'm sorry," I mutter. "I'm sorry." Overwhelmed with emotion, I sit on the bed and put my face in my hands to get a hold of myself. I fight the urge to cry.

"It's just I feel so helpless being so far away from her," I try to explain. "I can't lose her, Mom. I just can't."

"That's why you have to take your time," Mom says sensibly, folding a shirt. "I know I can't stop you from leaving, but I can at least help you get ready. Come on, Macy, let's go pack some food for Omaha's trip." They head downstairs together and I'm glad. It will be easier on Macy if she keeps busy. Macy and I are a lot alike.

Mom's right. As much as I just want to get out of here, it's foolish not to think through what I'll need for the days ahead. When I used to get impatient on a hunt, Grandpa would always say to me, "Only two things on earth rush, Omaha: rivers and fools. Which are you?"

I'm not a river or a fool so I obediently start with my backpack. Even though I used it for scouting, Dad always called it my bug-out bag. It's a phrase they use in the military when they have no other option but to evacuate and get out of Dodge. A bug-out bag contains everything you need to get from ground zero to a safe destination – or, in my case, from a safe destination to ground zero. My bug-out bag is an old external frame scout pack that belonged to Dad when he was a boy. Grandpa gave it to him when he earned First Class. It's been well used, but it's still in great shape. I've taken it on many treks into the woods and it's never failed me. The weathered light tan canvas looks better with age and I like that it still has the embroidered patches on the front flap from some of Dad's scout camporees.

I'm about to leave the familiarity of the farm for the war zone of Philadelphia. I'm going, but I admit it: I'm scared. Impulsively, I grab a permanent marker from my desk and carefully scribe the eagle wings symbol under his name.

"A scout is brave," I whisper. "I wish I was as brave as you."

I know that the best antidote to the jitters is action, so I turn my attention to packing what I'll need for the journey ahead.

"Shelter, water, fire and food," I say out loud as if someone is listening.

It's early spring so I don't have to worry about a heavy tent. Instead, I opt for my thick, waxed-canvas tarp. I can rig this tarp in countless shelter configurations and it offers more flexibility than a tent. I wrap my wool blanket inside the tarp and then lash it to the bottom of my pack with a piece of leather strapping. This blanket has kept me warm during many cold nights hunting elk in the mountains.

"Shelter: check," I announce.

Fresh drinking water is essential. Symptoms of dehydration

can set in within just a few hours if I'm not properly hydrated.
In extreme weather conditions, humans can live for three hours
without shelter, three days without water, and three weeks
without food. I plan on surviving no matter what, which means
I'm not taking any chances. I fill my stainless steel water bottle
in the bathroom and then pack it in one of the easy-access side
pockets on the pack. Once I use up this water I'll collect more
from a river or stream and then boil it in the metal bottle to
purify it for drinking. I also pack twenty-four water purification
tablets. I bought a case of these for the bunker a year ago from
a disaster supply company that was shut down when the WUG
took over. I figure these will come in handy if, for some reason,
I can't or don't want to light a fire.

"Water: check," I say, stuffing the tablets into the front flap
of my pack.

Grandpa taught me all of the old ways to make fire without
matches and modern tools, but I'll only use those methods
if I'm desperate. When my scout troop went on campouts, I
showed the others how to do it, and after a while the whole
troop got the hang of it. But right now, I'm packing an easy,
guaranteed way to start a fire: fire tinder made from cotton balls
coated heavily in petroleum jelly. They are cheap, really effective
and easy to make at home. I grow a small patch of cotton plants
in the meadow each year, just for this reason, so I don't have
to go into town. One petroleum jelly-soaked cotton seed pod
burns about seven minutes, which is plenty long enough to get
a fire started in not-so-perfect conditions. I take a few minutes
to mix up enough to fill a small leather pouch that London
made me from a piece of elk hide. I place this in the bottom of
my pack. I always keep my fire striker tied around my neck.

"Fire: check."

Lastly, I toss in a head-lamp flashlight; an atlas map that Dad used to keep in the seat pocket of the car; a small metal pot I made from an old coffee can; a camouflage rain poncho; several lengths of parachute cord; a large cotton bandanna; a small first aid kit; a compass; a compact pair of binoculars that Dad got while on a tour in Germany; a small folding Boy Scout pocket knife that belonged to Grandpa; and three extra pair of wool socks that Macy knitted for me last Christmas. Just as I tuck them away, Macy bursts through the door.

"We've packed food," she announces. "All of your favorites. There's a paper bag of wild turkey and elk jerky, a small loaf of homemade bread, some dried apple slices and a one-quart jar of Mom's pickled hard-boiled eggs."

She proceeds to stuff this into various pockets of my pack. I take this opportunity to grab several items that will help me catch my own food on the journey: a small fishing kit that I made to earn my fishing merit badge, a metal frog gig, a variety of wire small-game snares and the most effective hunting weapon I own, which is my slingshot.

This slingshot is my most prized possession. I still remember when Dad brought it home from his second-to-last tour in Asia. It was the last time he was home. As I hold the slingshot in my hand, where it fits perfectly, I remember Dad telling me that the Gi-Nong didn't use modern weapons or guns. They are a tribe whose native lands included a range of rain forest that happens to sit on top of one of the largest oil reserves in all of Asia. They didn't want Americans drilling on their land. It was the last straw. They went to war against us.

"I can't really blame them for defending their land," he'd told me once, privately. "And what we're doing over there – well, we need the oil, but it's hard on those people." I asked him why he didn't just stay home from now on and he looked sad and said, "I wish I could, Omaha. I truly wish I could. Just like the Scout Oath says, Son, we have a duty to God and our country." After a few seconds of thought, he added, "We also have a duty to our fellow man as well, Omaha."

Dad was tasked with heading the special units in charge of tracking and relocating the Gi-Nong. He said that even against troops with high-tech guns, heat-detection scopes and military survival supplies, the Gi-Nong were a nearly impossible force to overcome. He explained how their men, women and children were all masters of natural camouflage. He spoke with admiration about how they used silent weapons such as booby traps, blowguns, arrows and slingshots, and had managed to do more harm to U.S. troops in the jungle environment than any modern military force ever had. Dad knew a lot about the Gi-Nong and even taught me some of the language. The one phrase I will never forget is Dnoces Tnemdnema, which he pronounced No-sez Nem Neema. In Gi-Nong, this phrase means "If it's worth fighting for, it's worth dying for."

Dad also told me about how the general in charge of his unit had tried to convince some of the Gi-Nong prisoners to help hunt and track their own people, and that not a single one took the deal, despite offers of personal gain. He said the Gi-Nong were loyal to their people and would lay their lives on the line in a moment's notice to protect each other and their allies. Dad said his General resented the Gi-Nong for their loyalty.

Two weeks after Dad's last trip over there, three decorated military officers visited our house with the news that he had been killed in action by Gi-Nong enemy forces and that his body was unrecoverable. They told Mom he'd died a hero – whatever that means. I made a frame for the letter they presented to Mom and it's been hanging on my wall ever since.

***

GENERAL COMMAND
US FORCES, ASIAN HEADQUARTERS
GI-NONG DIVISION

Dear Ms. Hoyt,

It is with great regret that I write about the untimely death of your husband, Hunter Hoyt, on the field of battle against Gi-Nong enemies.

I can assure you that Hunter had selfless conviction for a cause that he considered to be greater than himself. In war, a man with conviction is the most formidable of all enemies, with a pursuit of purpose that would tire those without it.

Sincerely,
General Tacca
Commander, Gi-Nong Division, Asia

***

My slingshot came from a Gi-Nong warrior. It is unlike any slingshot I've ever seen: hand carved from an almost-black wood, it's shaped like a scorpion with the two pincers being the forks on which the red elastic bands attach. On the back of the scorpion is a large red circle. Macy said that the red circle looked evil so she embellished it with red paint to make it look like a rose instead. (She said it would always remind me of our password, Rugosa– like I could ever forget that!) The leather pouch that connects the two pieces of elastic can launch a variety of projectiles including rocks and lead balls. But the pouch also has a unique feature. On the top side is a small wire loop. Dad told me the Gi-Nong carve six-inch arrows, which they call munti, out of bamboo. They add a notch near the tip, which hooks on this wire loop. They use it to launch deadly, poison-tipped darts with pinpoint accuracy. Dad said they poison the munti by rubbing them on the back of a certain lizard in the jungle. He told stories of soldiers who died from being just barely grazed by a poisoned Gi-Nong munti. I make my own munti from black locust thorns. Not to brag, but I can shoot a squirrel through the eye from a distance of thirty yards without making a sound.

I don't know exactly how Dad came to acquire this slingshot. He never told me, but I imagine that he took it from a fallen enemy Gi-Nong warrior in combat. Dad would never talk about the men he had killed in battle. Once, Macy asked, but he never answered. He was like me – at least the way I hope I am: he didn't say much, but whatever he said mattered.

I quickly lash the slingshot to the outside of my pack and fill the large side pocket with my own munti and some round lead balls that I molded myself from scrap lead weights I pried off old car wheels in the junk yard near town. I glance at the clock and realize it's almost 8 p.m. This is one night I can't miss my chat with Rake. I hope he's logged on.

Before I leave my room, I remove a picture of London from the wooden frame I made for it so it could sit on my desk. I took that picture on the morning she left for Philadelphia. She's standing in the meadow with her back to the sun and her dark brown hair is cut to her shoulders and blowing in the early-summer wind. I've looked at this picture so many times I can see her silhouette with my eyes closed. We spent a lot of time in that meadow together growing up, but that day was different. For one thing, it was the only time I can ever remember being

sad there. The meadow was our place for good memories. I
wanted to disappear into the green wilderness that stretched
behind us. I wanted us to go away together and never come
back.

"Do you really have to go?" I'd asked her, already knowing
the answer.

"I have to go away for a while, Omaha," she'd said, looking
away from me. "I need a break from this place. You can come
visit me anytime you want."

"But why do you have to leave?" I'd regretted the whine in
my voice as soon as I said the words.

"You know how much I love you and Mom and Macy, but I
just need some space right now. Everything reminds me of him.
I'm too sad here."

Then she leaned over and gave me a slow kiss. I was so
surprised, so happy. It was just like I'd always dreamed it would
be, with her lips soft and her breath smelling lightly of mint tea.
I moved to put my arms around her, but she pulled away.

"I'm going," she said, a warning note in her voice.

"I understand," I said, trying to rein in all my feelings, to
be strong for her. "But listen to me, London: no matter what
happens, I will always be here for you."

And then she'd given me a look of amusement and said, "I
appreciate the sentiment, Omaha, but you don't have to worry
about me. I'll only be away for the summer."

"Even so," I'd said stubbornly, "I promise."

Now, two years later, I will make good on that promise.

CHAPTER THREE

I have one friend in the world besides London. I've never met him in person, but there's not much I don't know about him and vice versa. His name is Rake, he's a year older than I am, and we've been talking on the subnet since shortly after London left. He knows all about London, but I never told him London is in his city, Philadelphia. I consider him a true friend and I know he does me as well, but I guess I'm the jealous type and I never liked the idea of Rake meeting her and maybe London liking him more than she likes me. I know, that's immature, but it's the truth and I'm admitting it. Rake is easy to like. He enjoys people, unlike me. Also unlike me, he's an Eagle Scout. He was able to earn the rank before the WUG disbanded scouting. I think London always wanted me to be better with people. She would like Rake, and I don't like thinking about that.

But tonight, I will call in my first big favor. I will ask him to find London and keep her safe until I can get there.

I sit down at Dad's desk and open the small screen of his military communicator. They sent it to us with Dad's other belongings after he died, which I'm sure was an oversight. But soon after, the WUG disbanded the military, so I figure no one is going to come knocking on the door asking for it now.

Dad showed me how to use it to accesses an Internet within the Internet, called the Subnet. The military created it as a high-security communications pathway to send soldiers and contractors their orders. The WUG can't trace the bandwidth it uses and they haven't shut it down yet, which makes me believe they don't know about it. The device is solar powered and easy to hide if WUG officials ever come here. Over the last couple of years, the subnet has turned into a community of people who trade goods and share information. It's grown a lot and I'm sure the WUG will catch wind of it at some point, which is why I keep very low key.

When London moved to Philadelphia I was lonely so I ended up spending my evenings exploring the subnet. I hear a lot of rebels coordinating plans to rise up against the WUG, but that doesn't interest me. I don't think there's anything we can do about the WUG except try to survive for as long as possible, and I aim to keep Mom and Macy – and London – safe as long as I can. But I also found a few people on the subnet like myself who are trying to survive under the radar of the WUG. They call themselves "survivalists," which I guess is what I am, too. I spent most of my time in the scouting corridor talking with other boy scouts. There's a corridor for almost any interest or trade now. This where I met Rake. He isn't really a rebel or a survivalist, but he is an Eagle Scout and I know I can trust him. He's also a technical genius who is curious about everything. For example, he hacked into the subnet using an old video game console.

I log on as OmahaH at 7:58 p.m., hoping he's there already. He's not. 8:09p.m. Still no sign of Rake. He's normally not late. Did the WUG find a way to shut down the subnet in Philadelphia? I remind myself that Rake is pretty resourceful with technology.

The subnet can be a seedy place and it's hard to know for sure whom you're talking to or whether they can be trusted, but I knew from the beginning that Rake was a good guy. I was following some chatter about some scouts who were planning a swap meet at an abandoned summer camp when, suddenly, a private message popped up on my screen from someone named Rake.

```
Rake:      OmahaH, H is for Hello?
OmahaH:    ??
Rake:      Seriously, though, thanks for the sandwich.
OmahaH:    I think you've got the wrong guy.
Rake:      No, you're definitely the guy.
OmahaH:    No, I'm not.
Rake:      Yes, you are. How can you have a name like
           that and not know?
OmahaH:    Know what?
Rake:      About my favorite sandwich.
```

I remember thinking at this point that Rake was just another one of the crazy subnetters who somehow ended up in the scouting corridor.

```
OmahaH:    No clue what you're talking about.
Rake:      My favorite sandwich was invented in Omaha,
           so thanks.
OmahaH:    I've never even been to Omaha.
Rake:      Doesn't matter. The Reuben is my favorite
           sandwich of all time. I actually wish I had
```

```
                 one now, but a conversation with you will
                 have to do. From now on your name is Reuben.
       OmahaH:   You're crazy.
       Rake:     Maybe so, Reuben Omaha. But let's assume I
                 am just a guy who appreciates an excellent
                 sandwich and this conversation is perfectly
                 sane.
```

That's how my first conversation with Rake went. He struck up another conversation the next night, and the next, and soon I was looking forward to his unpredictable, sometimes brilliant comments. I've come to learn that he can be funny and smart, but he also has a serious side. He's been looking for his parents for over a year. They were sent to the work camps when he was 17. He was assigned to a foster center and ran away after one day. He's been squatting in an abandoned apartment building in Philadelphia ever since. He managed to create a fake WUG ID for himself and is able to live off stolen credits and helping people gain access to the subnet. After we'd been friends for a few months he confided that the only thing that keeps him going is his quest to find his parents. That's why he spends so much time scanning the subnet and trying to network there; he's hoping to hear something about the work camps. We all wonder what goes on there. It's hard to separate out truth from speculation and rumor.

Rake has always been curious about who I am and the details of my life. I tell him about hunting elk and setting traps. He likes to hear what I've caught and eaten every day. He says it sounds a lot tastier than the WUG rations, which is some kind of tasteless soy protein. He was a city scout in Philadelphia. I guess city scouts do city stuff. It was hard to imagine that he'd only been on a few campouts. His troop did things like clean up the city parks and help distribute food to the homeless. His favorite merit badge was Electronics. Mine was Wilderness Survival. No one in his troop earned Wilderness Survival! I think Wilderness Survival should be a Boy Scout requirement, especially for an Eagle Scout. Regardless, maybe as friends go, opposites attract. I must be rubbing off on him though because last year, he decided to make his own survival bunker in the basement of his apartment building, in a hollow wall behind a storage compartment. I told him how to store water and how to preserve foods for long-term storage, and I also helped him figure out a way to pipe air into the bunker and create a waste system using ground up newspapers and kitty litter. He told me he's moved blankets, flashlights, batteries, and other supplies in there over the last year, including mattresses. It's not a fortified bunker by any means, but it will be a place to hide if all hell breaks loose.

I remember that all hell has already broken loose. Where is Rake? I drum on the desk impatiently. Where is he?

8:17p.m. Just as I'm about to give up on him and log off, Rakes pops online and I breathe a sigh of relief.

Rake:	reuben???
OmahaH:	rake, thank god! u ok?
Rake:	i didn't make it out in time. i'm freakin trapped here reuben. i'm in the bunker, like a rat in a hole. Subnet device power is fading. not sure how long I can stay connected.
OmahaH:	i need your help
Rake:	??
OmahaH:	London is in Philly, too. she's all alone. i am on my way but won't get there for three days. will you keep her safe until i can get to you?

```
Rake:       WHAT??!! YOU CAN'T COME HERE REUBEN! it's
            suicide! we're all dead here, just like the
            people in the other cities the WUG punished.
            i'm sorry about London. I know you love her.
            why didn't you tell me london was here???
```

I ignore his question.

```
OmahaH:     I AM coming there and none of us are going
            to die. i need u and london to stay alive
            until i get there. i only have enough fuel
            to make it part way and then I'll have to
            walk the last 70 miles so i think i can be
            there in 3 to 4 days. rake, you gotta make
            it man. you have to.
```

There is a long pause and I have stopped breathing. Finally, his message appears.

```
Rake:       where is she?
OmahaH:     second floor above London Leather at 623
            leslie street.
Rake:       even if i can find her, we won't last much
            longer than 3 days. the city is falling
            apart fast and the WUG soldiers are running
            firing squads all morning for people they
            catch on the streets.
OmahaH:     i will be there. please go get her now. i
            need to know she's safe. tell her omaha sent
            you. use the password RUGOSA. she probably
            still has some dried elk jerky that i sent
            her.
```

Another pause, and I imagine Rake thinking hard about what I'm asking.

```
Rake:       it's totally crazy, but why not? it's not
            too far if I run across the rooftops when
```

```
it gets dark. their heat detectors are all
street level, so i should be able to stay
clear of the soldiers.
```

Relief floods through me. I don't deserve this kind of friend.

```
OmahaH:   rake, i swear I will be there in time to get
          you and London out. stay strong!
Rake:     you too Rueben. good luck life scout. you
          know this eag--
```

The connection is broken and he's gone. I feel stunned. He's really going to do it. We have a plan in place, and now it's up to me to rescue them both. I am going to cross the state of Pennsylvania, somehow find a way to sneak into quarantined Philadelphia and rescue my friends. And I have four days at most before the bombs flatten the city.

A sudden rush of adrenaline sends me outside in the dark. I sprint to the barn and throw the tarp off my dirt bike. I haven't used it in a year. I'd been saving it to trade for a couple of goats or pigs, but it will be perfect for the first part of this trip, until I run out of fuel and have to abandon it and go on foot. I rifle through a box on Dad's workbench and find the dark-green, black and brown spray paint cans. I give the dirt bike a soldier's makeover. I spray the bright yellow gas tank and fenders solid black and put a coat of brown on the chrome headlight and handlebars. Using a small branch of maple leaves as a template, I spray the dark green paint to stencil a break-up pattern all over the bike – even the tires. My biggest threat on this trip is being caught by WUG officials. I'm not allowed to travel without a WUG ID, and if I'm caught they'll ship me off to a work camp without a second thought. I decide I'll die before I let them make me a slave.

I siphon gas out of the tractor and truck to fill the dirt bike's gas tank plus two small gas cans, which I lash to the tiny wire rack above the rear tire. I take a few minutes to spray paint those as well. It's more than 400 miles to Philadelphia and I should be able to make it 350 miles or so with the amount of gas I have. But I absolutely can't risk taking the highway, which is busy with the WUG convoys. I'll stick to the back roads to avoid WUG checkpoints. Back roads will have far fewer people, and the fewer people I encounter the better. Any one of them might decide to turn me in for a reward. The thought makes my stomach sour.

It's late by the time I finish prepping the bike, but I need to have everything ready to leave at first light, and there's one last important task at hand. There is no way I'm going to attempt this journey without packing some kind of lethal ammunition. I've decided I'll use my munti in the same way the Gi-Nong do – dipped in lethal poison. But we don't have poison lizards here in the West Virginia. What we do have is monkshood. When I was just a little boy, Grandpa showed me the wildflower and demonstrated how his ancestors boiled the root in water to make poisonous syrup that they used to hunt wild game. They dipped the tips of arrows into it and used blowguns to shoot down their prey. He warned me never to touch the plant, and made sure I didn't mistake it for another plant that has a similar flower and is edible. He gravely told me that his cousin misidentified monkshood and died after eating just one leaf.

There's only one place I know for sure monkshood grows, and it's a place I planned on visiting before my departure anyway. So I grab an empty metal soup can and an old glass jelly jar from the barn and head up the ridge behind our house to the forest clearing. My flashlight lights up the familiar trail through the woods.

As always, I stop along the way to admire my favorite tree. It's a big beech with smooth, silver bark. Grandpa called it the Tree of Memories. It has an ominous look under the moonlight, but it represents only happiness for my family. We've all carved pictures and words on the tree to remind us of happy times. Dad carved a big heart when Macy was born. Mom carved a little fox when we found Tunnel. Macy carved an arrow when she made her first bow. London carved the words Love & Leather. I carved a line each time Grandpa and I brought back an elk for the winter. Just seeing the many carvings makes me smile. All of them represent a good memory. I trace a few of the older ones with my finger and then shine my light high up in the tree to see my happiest one of all. It's an O + L that London and I carved years ago.

"Sorry old friend," I say to the tree. "I've got nothing good to carve today. I'll have plenty to carve about when I get back, though."

As I peak the hill before the clearing, I can already see in the moonlight the purple monkshood flowers a few yards ahead where we buried Dad and Grandpa. The distinct flowers decorate the gravesites as if they had been planted on purpose, but I know the monkshood grew there on its own. I cut a sharp digging stick from a fallen maple branch and carefully begin to pry up the earth around one of the largest flower stalks. Even under the light of my flashlight I can see the root is a deep maroon color. It reeks with a pungent odor that burns my nostrils. I push it into the metal can with the stick and then quickly gather six more, being very cautious not to touch the plant or root with my bare hands. I scoop up about a half cup of water from a spring that runs down the ridge past the graves and add it to the can of roots, and then I clear a spot for my fire.

I peel a handful of dry inner bark from a big dead cottonwood tree and bring it to flame with just one spark from the ferro rod I wear on a leather thong around my neck. The fibrous inner bark of the cottonwood tree is one of nature's best fire-starting tinders. The fire lights up our private forest graveyard and shadows dance around me with every flicker of flame. I feel alert to the noises of the night critters, but I'm not afraid. The dark of night in the woods is a kind of holiness for me, who grew up learning to love and appreciate and respect the wild.

It's not nature that worries me. I can deal with nature. Nature has a certain order to her. Nature takes only what she needs, motivated by sheer survival. Nothing in nature takes more than it needs to survive. It's people that worry me. Their motivations are often rooted in greed and desire for control, with a complete disregard for life and balance. On this journey, I will stay as close to nature and as far from people as I possibly can.

In a few minutes the contents of my small metal can comes to a rolling boil. As the monkshood roots soften, I smash them in the bottom of the can with a blunt stick to release every last bit of deadly toxins. It boils down to a deep purple syrup that smells sharp and tart. I turn my head away so I don't inhale too much of the poison. Plants nearby visibly wilt as the purple haze creeps out of the boiling bubbles in my can. I use my bandanna to hold the hot can, and I carefully pour the death syrup into the old jelly jar and seal it with a twist of the lid.

"Just like Grandma used to make," I say aloud with smile.

I shine the flashlight on the faded, handwritten label: "Grape

Jelly." It really does look exactly like Grandma's wild grape jelly. There is no time to test my poison on large game, and that worries me some.

"I hope this works," I say with my hand on Grandpa's gravestone.

I may not be fearless, but with Grandpa's poison and Dad's slingshot, I suddenly feel like I have a fighting chance at bringing London home.

By the time I get back to the house it is well after midnight and I'm completely exhausted, but ready for my journey. Macy is asleep on the couch and I cover her with a quilt on my way upstairs, which stirs her awake.

"Omaha," she whispers sleepily. "Don't leave before saying good bye. I made something for you to take."

"Don't worry," I reply. "I won't. Go back to sleep."

Exhausted, I crash on my bed. I want to leave this minute, but I know I need at least a few hours of sleep. Eyes closed, I whisper an old prayer that Grandpa always said before a hunt:

If we are lost, guide our steps.
If we are shaken, steady our sights.
If we are alone, comfort our soul.
Finally, if we are worthy, take us home.

Grandpa used to tell me stories about how the ancestors work through nature to help us. Once, when he was a boy of about ten, he was off hunting by himself and was bitten by a rattlesnake. Alone in the forest, delirious and barely conscious, he battled the venom for six days. He said the only reason he survived was because forest animals brought him everything he needed. The birds positioned leaves so that rain and dew dripped into his dry mouth when he was thirsty. Squirrels dropped nuts for him to eat when he was hungry. Fox and raccoon laid with him in the freezing cold to keep him warm at night. When the venom finally ran its course, he was able to make it home.

Just before I drift off, I pray: "God, please send Dad and Grandpa to help me and London make it back home."

***

I wake suddenly to the sound and smell of sizzling bacon in the kitchen. The sun is not yet up, but I'm mad at myself for sleeping this long. Why hasn't Mom woken me? I had horrible dreams. All night I was being chased by Gi-Nong warriors who wished to avenge the deaths of their relatives who Dad had killed. As I drink the cold water Mom left by my bed the night before, I remind myself that at least there will be no Gi-Nong in Philadelphia.

Even though it's spring, the nights are still chilly. I hurriedly pull on my whipcord wool pants, a brown thermal shirt and an olive-drab canvas vest that London made from an old military tarp. I lace up the moccasins London gave me and wrap a buckskin scarf around my neck. I remove my Dad's Eagle Scout patch from the wooden display board on my wall and put it in my pocket for good luck. Lastly, I strap on my belt and machete and pull over a thick wool military shirt-jack Dad wore while in service. It still has his name patch on the chest pocket - H. HOYT. H stands for Hunter, which was Dad's first name. The weight of my bug-out bag feels good on my shoulders. I like the feeling of suiting up for a journey. When I come into the kitchen, Mom switches off the TV.

"What?" I ask.

"Oh, it's nothing you need to be watching right now," she

says, her mouth tight with worry.

"Philadelphia is getting worse," I say, dread in my gut.

"They're going from home to home and pulling people outside and lining them up."

She doesn't say, but I already know: people are being killed by firing squads. We saw it happen in all the other big cities. I fervently hope Rake got to London last night.

I sit down and start bolting down a plate of bacon, eggs and drop biscuits. I'd rather not even take the time to eat, but I do it anyway out of respect for Mom. Macy wanders in from the living room wrapped in a blanket. She and Mom are clearly distraught, but neither one says anything. I know their chances of surviving, if I don't come back, are not great. I'm the main provider of food for our family. But they love London, too.

"Macy, you're in charge of getting the bunker stocked while I'm gone," I say, because she's looking at me with such despair and I can't stand it. "I'm counting on you, okay?"

"Okay," she answers in a small voice.

"Okay?" I ask again, raising my eyebrows a little.

She straightens up and looks me in the eye. "Yeah, Omaha. You can count on me."

"I cut a path to the entrance. It's not obvious, but you'll see it if you really look. Pull back branches just to the left of the big boulder and you'll see the path I cut. Don't make more than one trip there per day, otherwise you'll start to make a trail." I know she already knows this, but I give her instructions anyway. "Take over some of the canned food that you and Mom put up in the root cellar. Fill the empty spaces on the shelves with as much dried jerky as will fit."

"What about water?" asks Mom.

"You won't need to store any water," I reply. "I installed

a hand pump that taps into an underground spring. We'll have all the fresh water we want. But be sure to pack in some blankets and all the plastic bags you can get your hands on. We may have to store waste for days at a time and we'll need those if we do. Everything else should already be in there."

They follow me outside to where my dirt bike is waiting. It's time to get on the road. My heart is racing, as if it wants to get to Philadelphia first.

"Here," Macy holds out her hand toward me. "I made a gift for London." I reach for it and see that it's a butterfly hair clip.

Macy pulls her hand back and says, "Be careful, Omaha, it's not just any butterfly hair clip."

"Oh really?" I reply. I want to get going, but play along for her sake.

"Yes," she says with a sly smile. "It's a survival butterfly hair clip. I filed the wing tips to be razor sharp."

In a quick motion she slices off a shaving of wood from the edge of the barn door.

"And I polished the underside to shine like a mirror so she can use it as a reflective rescue signal." She demonstrates by shining a reflection into my eyes from the sliver of morning sun that's just rising.

"I wrapped the body with 10 feet of fishing line and glued on two fishing hooks for antenna," she concludes proudly.

Just when I think the presentation is over, Macy draws her hand back and flings the butterfly pin inside the barn door. I hear a shrill cry as the butterfly finds its mark – a mouse creeping along the feed bin.

"And, it's a throwing weapon," Macy announces, clearly pleased with herself.

As we make eye contact, I realize that the kid sister I used to know has grown up and hardened somehow into this person. I love her so much, but I feel sad. She should be playing with dolls, not figuring out how to make deadly survival weapons from hairpins. Regardless, I can't help but be impressed. It really looks like a harmless butterfly hair clip.

"London will love it," I say, squeezing Macy tightly against me. "She is going to be so impressed with how much you've grown in two years."

"I have to go," I say, untangling myself from Macy. "Take care of Mom. And check Mr. Pine by the pond later. He may have dinner waiting for you."

Fighting back tears, Mom hugs me and whispers, "Omaha, you come back to me. I can't lose you too. Neither of us can."

"I'm coming back, Mom, but it might be a few weeks. I'll be ditching the bike on the way there and then we'll have to walk the whole way back, but I will be home," I promise. "If you guys feel like you're in any danger at all, go straight to the bunker and don't look back. You can survive in there for a long time. But don't worry, okay? I'll be back before your tomato plants come up."

She smiles, but she and I both know I can't guarantee anything. It's unspoken of course, but we are all scared this is the last time we'll see each other.

I secure the bag on my back, start the bike and give a last wave, and then I aim east. Finally, I'm on my way. The wind pushes my tears back toward the house, which shrinks in the distance behind me. It's been more than two years since I've traveled farther than town, and I already miss my forest and pond and meadow. I'm the only one on the paved road as I coast through town in the gray light of dawn. I hardly give it a look, but even through the corner of my eye I can see all the boarded-up shops and empty buildings. Homesickness fills me for a minute, and then I push it away. I need to focus on the here and now. I'm unregistered, traveling without a UNIM ID or a travel permit, and I'm carrying weapons. The reality of my situation courses through my veins, but there is no going back. I'm worried, but I also feel relief knowing I am on my way.

My fears of being captured by WUG soldiers fade a bit once I turn off pavement and get on the back roads that wind their way toward the Pennsylvania border. Old logging roads and country lanes are empty most times, and especially early in the morning. As the sun burns stronger, I take in the beauty of nature around me. The mountains, at this time of the year, are absolutely stunning and abundant with flowers and wild edibles. I daydream that London is with me on this bike and the WUG doesn't exist, and we're heading to the ocean for vacation. The more I think about her, the more I twist the accelerator in my right hand and the faster I go.

As I round a big s-curve out of the valley my daydreaming is over. About a hundred yards in front of me is a huge WUG military transport vehicle. It's parked diagonally to block the entire road. My heart sinks. I had counted on there being no WUG presence on the road this far into the countryside. Two armed soldiers see me and they step into the road and raise their hands, signaling me to stop.

If I stop, they will capture me. If I continue, they will shoot me. If I turn around, they will chase me. With only a split second to react, I jerk the handlebars sharply to the left and ramp the embankment.

CHAPTER FOUR

The briar bushes and brambles rip at my clothes and face as I tear through the overgrowth beside the large open field of the valley. I hear shouting in a foreign language and then gunfire. My front fender explodes into pieces as a bullet tears through it. I lean forward into the bike and hear another round burst through my bug-out bag and hiss over my left shoulder. I feel liquid pouring down my back and panic for a minute thinking it's blood. It's too cold to be blood, I think. It's the water from my stainless steel bottle. But then I feel something hot and strange on my arm and my bike starts to slow down. A growing red stain catches my eye and I feel something warm running down my right arm. My hand is covered with blood and my grip on the accelerator is slipping. I quickly wipe the grip clean with the cuff of my shirt and wrench down on the accelerator again, lurching the bike forward.

As I head over the small knoll, I dart a look back to assess my enemies. The hill is temporarily hiding me from view, but

as soon as they crest it I will be an easy target. I can hear them
shouting in the distance. They are headed my way on foot, but I
doubt they can outrun my bike. I speed toward the picket fence
that separates the meadow from the forest and valley below. I
screech to a stop and leap off, abandoning the bike to jump the
fence and race through the woods and down the ridge to the
valley. I stop to catch my breath and to pull an old bandanna
from my pocket and tie it tightly around the cuff on my right
arm. I don't want my blood to spill and leave my pursuers a
trail to follow. I try to fight back the panic. Armed soldiers are
chasing me, but I remind myself that I'm not exactly helpless.

Dad and I would often hunt wild game using only natural
camouflage, and I know for a fact that if I can hide from the
animals that live in the forest, I can hide from these WUG
soldiers. Dad spent many hours teaching me the natural
camouflage techniques of the Gi-Nong. He told countless
stories of how Gi-Nong warriors would kill U.S. soldiers from
just a few feet away. With these stories racing through my mind,
I take off my bug-out bag and dive almost headfirst into the
muddy creek bed at the bottom of the valley. I quickly slather
my entire body with slick, gooey creek mud. I scramble up
the embankment and roll around intently on the forest floor,
ignoring the searing pain in my arm.

Omaha slowly disappears and a creature of leaves, sticks
and forest debris rises from the ground. I unlash the slingshot
from my bag and grab a handful of munti and my jar of fresh
monkshood jelly. I fling my bug-out bag as hard as I can in
the direction of the WUG soldiers. It lands about fifteen yards
away and will be the perfect decoy to grab their attention. I
sneak down the creek and take shelter under a huge stand of
overhanging ostrich ferns. Then I quickly dip five munti in jelly.

My hands tremble in fear and I try to steady them as best I can. I load one in my slingshot and wait. My heart pounds in my chest. I can't believe this is happening. I can hear the words of my Grandfather, "A scout is fearless."

The two WUG soldiers come barreling over the hilltop on foot. They don't even hesitate as they jump the fence where I ditched my bike. I note that they're both a lot bigger than I am, and they're both armed with assault rifles and neither one looks winded. When they cross the forest edge the one in front signals the other one to slow down and they search for signs of me. They're stalking me like I'm wild game, searching for my trail. They think I'm still on the run. Little do they know that I am now hunting them. The first soldier wears a wool coat that is too thick for my wooden munti to puncture, even at close range. My shot placement must be absolutely perfect on the first attempt. The other wears an unbuttoned long-sleeve shirt, which leaves his chest completely exposed.

"Es ist sein rucksack," one of the soldiers states as he points to my bag. A lot of German mercenaries work for the WUG. Germany used to be our ally. I feel anger growing in my chest.

As they cautiously approach my bug-out bag, the second soldier clumsily replaces the magazine in his rifle. I take advantage of this distracting moment and quietly position the slingshot and draw my first munti. They are well within shooting range. I've taken squirrel at this distance many times before. However, there has never been a second squirrel with a machine gun to avenge the first one. Before my first munti even finds its target I must have the second loaded for a follow-up shot.

A scout is brave! I silently command myself, even though my heart pounds with terror.

For a split second my mind flashes back to the last time I was with Dad. He insisted we take a walk through the pine valley. He was leaving for Asia that afternoon. The pine valley is a place filled with old-growth white pines and strewn with boulders the size of small cars. The needle bed prevents all other plants from growing and the wind makes a deep purring sound as it rushes through the boughs hundreds of feet above the bronze-carpeted floor. Even on the hottest summer days, the meandering creek cools the valley with ground water from the mountain peaks above and the crisp smell of pine resin overpowers all other scents in the forest.

"Son," he'd said, "true bravery is not the absence of fear. Fear is your ally. It heightens your senses and awareness. Being brave means you use fear to make better decisions. Manage your fears, Omaha, and you can manage any situation, no matter how difficult."

As the first soldier kneels down to pick up my bug-out bag, I imagine a squirrel sleeping across his neck. Without hesitation, I silently launch a poison-tipped munti deep into his exposed throat. Before he can react, I've already taken aim at the second soldier, making the split-second decision to go for a no-risk chest shot where his shirt in unbuttoned. This shot finds its mark just seconds after the first soldier gurgles a horrible scream of shock and pain. Neither of them has any idea what has hit them or where it came from, but they are still clutching their guns so I stay crouched and motionless beneath the large fern fronds, cloaked in mud and forest debris.

As the first soldier stumbles around in a panicked stupor I launch a third munti aimed at the second soldier's inner thigh, hoping to connect with the femoral artery that runs there. The faster I get monkshood jelly in their blood stream, the sooner this is over, I hope. My direct hit sends him reeling. He loses his footing on the hillside, tumbles down the ridge and lands just a few feet from where I'm hiding. I quickly scan the hillside to make sure no other soldiers are joining the party. So far, it seems like there are only these two. That's good. I carefully draw my machete to finish off the second soldier, but I can tell it isn't going to be necessary. He is already vomiting a purple-colored mess and can barely take a breath. I step out from my fern canopy and pull the rifle from his hands just in case. He stops breathing and thrashing. I can't look away. This is the first man I've ever killed. The purple, bloodshot veins in his eyes are a sight that will haunt me forever.

Soldier number one lies motionless on the ridge next to my pack. He is the second man I've killed. I take a deep breath and then another. I notice the forest is silent again. Mother Nature is neutral in this war.

I've never killed a man before. Killing animals to support my family is different. It doesn't bother me. I feel grateful to the animals whose lives give us continued life, and out of respect to them nothing goes to waste from those kills. We eat the meat or use it to barter for other goods to keep us alive. We use the hide for leather or fur. I sell the bones to be ground up for livestock feed. I make glue from the hooves and even feed the entrails to our pigs. But this killing is so different. I want nothing from these men I've killed. A sick feeling surges through my gut. The reality of what's just happened is hard to process. I feel exhausted, spacey. I suddenly understand why my Dad would never answer questions about what he did in the jungles. It isn't something you want to talk about or even think about. The silence and faint smell of vomit from the soldiers makes me feel lightheaded and I struggle to keep down my breakfast.

"I had no choice," I hear myself explaining to the dead soldier in front of me. "I'm sorry, but you gave me no choice. I didn't want this, but you gave me no choice."

They didn't give me a choice. They would have killed me or enslaved me. I had to do it and I know I'd better come to grips right now with the fact that I might have to do it again. There's no going back. This is the reality of the journey: it's kill or be killed. Scouts don't kill people, but I had no choice. I straighten up and look away from the dead man. Dying isn't an option. I have to get to London and nothing – and no one – is going to get in my way.

I suddenly sway on my feet and become fully aware of the searing pain in my right forearm where I was shot. I untie the bandanna and pull up my sleeve to find a three-inch-long open gash across the top of my arm. The bullet just grazed me, but it's still a very deep flesh wound. I climb the ridge to fetch my bug-out bag, stepping over the dead man, to find my first aid kit. I walk back down to the stream and wash off as best I can, and then I dress the cleaned wound with antiseptic and bandages. Luckily this kit is waterproof because when the bullet shredded my metal canteen, all my gear is soaking wet.

I decide to leave the soldiers where they are, but I also decide to loot anything I think I can use from them. This includes a bolt-action sniper rifle with a box of 24 bullets; a metal canteen to replace my own; a .22 caliber revolver pistol with a small belt-dump pouch of ammunition; an olive-colored wool hat; and a fixed-blade belt knife. I repack my gear and cautiously creep to the top of the hill, using my binoculars to scan the vehicle from which they came. The doors are open and there doesn't seem to be any more soldiers, which is odd. Their transport vehicle is enormous. Maybe they are on their way to collect work camp slaves. I watch for a few minutes just in case. Two civilian cars drive tentatively around the transport. No one will dare to stop for a WUG vehicle unless they see a soldier holding an automatic rifle flagging them down.

I retrieve my bike and decide to dig a hole at the base of a big maple tree standing majestically in the middle of the field and bury the sniper rifle because it's so bulky. I wrap the rifle and ammunition in one of the soldier's thick vinyl ponchos and mark the spot with a big rock. I doubt I'll ever be back in this area, but you just never know. Grandpa used to hide caches of tools and supplies in caves on long hunting trips and I've used items from his caches years later, even after he had passed. I've even hidden a few of my own throughout the mountains around our home.

There are no cars approaching, so I decide it's safe enough to look through the WUG vehicle for resources, but of course I approach it very carefully. Big white letters on the side of the truck identify it as WUG Transport 6478. Why is it here? I guess it broke down, which means the soldiers must have radioed for help. Another WUG caravan could be arriving any moment. Goosebumps run up my spine with the thought of encountering more WUG soldiers. I move as fast as I can, pulling myself into the front passenger seat. There is a first aid kit mounted on the door. I rummage through it and take supplies to restock my own kit. I also take a vile of penicillin and a syringe. I use the latex tourniquet tubing from their kit and quickly siphon gas from the WUG vehicle to refill the small tank on my dirt bike. I wish I had a way to store more of it – extra fuel can save me days of walking. I grab two Military Meals Ready to Eat (MREs) from the back seat and shove them in my bug-out bag. The packaging is in German so I guess they will be mystery meals for later. I also decide to take a hand-held, scanner-looking gizmo that seems like it might be useful, though I don't know exactly what it is. Just as I'm weighing whether or not it's worth taking, a voice over the hand held radio clipped above the sun visor breaks the silence and I flinch.

"Wir sind zehn Meilen von sechs-vier-sieben-acht," the voice reports.

I don't remember much from high school German class and Dad's lessons, but I do remember numbers and meilen sounds like miles.

"Ten miles from 6-4-7-8," I translate aloud. I need to get out of here now.

I grab the radio off the visor and clip it to the shoulder strap of my bug-out bag as I make my way to the rear of the vehicle. I throw open the rear door and am caught completely off guard by a huge German Shepherd dog, which lunges at me from inside a cramped cage. It surprises me so much I nearly fall backward, but my attention immediately shifts to what lies next to the cage: a dead girl. It looks as if she's just been tossed into the back of the truck like a sack of potatoes. Her body is in an awkward, unorganized heap. Seeing her like this, a flush of anger surges through my body and I'm glad I killed those two soldiers. My stomach starts to churn and I can't help but throw up on the side of the road. When I finish, I turn my attention back to the girl. She's beautiful. She has stark blonde hair and pale skin. She looks to be about my age. I pause for a second, wishing I could do something for her. I wish I could give her a proper burial, but I know I don't have time. The WUG rescue crew will be here soon.

I slam the back door. Just as it closes I think I see her chest move. Is my mind playing tricks on me or did I just really see that? I didn't check her pulse. Is my own blood loss making me see things? I open the door and quickly press two fingers across her carotid artery.

"Oh my God!" I gasp. "You're alive."

A mix of emotions rushes through my mind. I need to find London and don't have time to help someone I don't even know. How do I know I can trust her? How am I supposed to take her with me anyway? I've got more than my fair share of problems already. This journey isn't about saving other people; it's about saving London. I slam the door and head in the direction of my bike, but after a few steps I turn around. A scout is helpful. I can't bring myself to leave the girl.

"I don't need this," I mutter. "I should just go!"

I run around to the front of the truck and cram the rest of the WUG first aid kit in my pack. I grab a long woolen overcoat from the back seat and wrap the girl inside it. Then I roll my bike over and, sitting on it, lift her onto it in front of me. I use the sleeves from the overcoat to tie her to me. My wounded arm protests with hot stabs of pain, and even after she's secure enough I have to hold her to keep her from flopping off. The whole time I'm aware that more soldiers are going to be on us any minute. I twist the grip to full throttle, which shoots even more pain through my arm, and then I take off down the road. But I'm so nervous I will see the WUG rescue squad coming right toward me that I turn randomly down the first back road I see. Just before the main road fades out of sight I look back and see the faint outline of a big military truck headed in the direction of the stranded transport. I break out in a sweat. It won't be long before they figure out what has happened. I focus on keeping the girl upright and not crashing us into the trees we are whipping by as I race down the gravel back road.

As I drive, I calculate that I've only lost half an hour, but it seems like a lifetime ago that I killed those soldiers. I feel the press of urgency and frustration that I don't know if this road is even going the right way. It's taking me more south than east, and I need to go east. I stop an hour down the road and feel better after I've mapped out my new route, which will take me on smaller back roads than I'd planned on taking. But I'd rather not meet any more WUG soldiers. I top off my gas tank from one of my small saddle tanks and swallow a few aspirin from the WUG first aid kit. My arm is killing me.

There is no change with the girl on my lap. I verify that she's still breathing and I re-tie the overcoat arms so she's more secure, and on we drive. As the sun starts to fade behind me, I decide it's time to stop for the night. I'd drive through the night if I was alone, but I have to see about the unconscious girl. I know it's not noble or kind, but I resent the delay. I pull off the road and lie her down in the leaves while I hide my bike in a thicket and cover it with dried grasses. Then I hoist her over my shoulder in a fireman's carry and hike deep into the dark woods. I tried to spare my wounded arm from bearing the brunt of her weight, and luckily she's not that heavy, but the pain in my arm makes me grit my teeth and it's shrieking at me by the time I find a place to set up camp. I prop her up against a tree and tell her I'll be right back, even though she's still unconscious. Then I walk back out and get my bug-out bag and hike back to her.

The girl is still unconscious as I set up a lean-to using a huge, fallen oak tree as our back wall. My arm feels like it is on fire with pain, but I gingerly set up my tarp as a canopy over the old oak and drag some pine boughs underneath to make a bed wide enough for both of us to share my one blanket. The situation might be more awkward if she was conscious, but I don't think about that much. Instead, I swear, because when I open the tarp all the way I discover that the bullet shot through it. There are eight evenly spaced holes in a diagonal line across the canopy. At least it doesn't look like it will rain today.

Under the light of my headlamp, I clean and dress my wound. It's a worrisome red color, so I smear antibiotic cream all around it and wrap it in clean bandages. Then I clean the wound on the blonde girl's head. She has scrapes and gashes on her arms and legs, but nothing serious. I notice a UPC code tattooed on her wrist just below a pea-sized bump under the skin. I remember the scanner device and immediately dig it out of my pack and push the big green button on top. It makes a loud beep.

The LED screen pops on and casts a mellow green hue into the darkness behind me. I cautiously hold up her wrist and pull the trigger. A red laser line appears on her arm and I draw it across the UPC tattoo. Two sharp BEEPS indicate a successful scan and the screen populates with information.

The girl in the photo on the scanner looks much healthier than the gaunt figure that lies nearly lifeless next to me. It's definitely the same girl, but there's no doubt this photo was taken some time ago. I read the information spooling up.

```
Name:     Nalim Reheuas
Origin:   USA
DOB:      5/3/YEAR UNKNOWN
Status:   Relocating to UNIM WEST Work Camp for
          interrogations
```

Today is May 2nd. Her birthday is tomorrow. She certainly

doesn't look like a criminal.

"I guess at this point any enemy of the WUG is a friend of mine," I whisper and pull the green wool overcoat up over her shoulders. "Even though you are slowing me down," I add.

I can't help wondering what this girl was doing in the back of that WUG vehicle. Where were they taking her? What had she done wrong? Why was she being relocated for questioning? The mellow green hue on the canopy suddenly changes to flashing red. My eyes dart to the scanner, which now flashes FUGITIVE-FUGITIVE-FUGITIVE in big red letters across the screen.

I press the green button again and everything fades to black. They know she has escaped. They probably think she killed the two German soldiers and they are certainly hunting for her. I should have just left her! I don't need this extra baggage. I need to get to Philadelphia so that I can help Rake and London escape. As usual, my thoughts turn to London. I hope she's safe. I hope they are both safely tucked away in Rake's bunker. With my mind racing and trying to process today's events I lay my head back against the big comforting oak and doze off to sleep.

I dream of our meadow. London and I have disappeared from the rest of the world and it's just the two of us lying among the wildflowers and songbirds. It's so real—she is talking in detail about what her shop will be like and I am thinking that when she stops talking I will kiss her. And just as I think I'll do it, I'm awakened by a blood-curdling scream from the stark blonde girl at my side.

CHAPTER FIVE

It takes me a second to figure out where I am. Not in the meadow with London. I'm in the woods with the damaged blonde girl, and she is screaming and thrashing around in what seems to be a horrible nightmare.

I stifle my irritation and disappointment that she's not London, and then I click on my headlamp and shake her gently. "Wake up now. It's okay. You're safe."

Her eyes pop open and I'm staring into pools of deep blue. Then she shrieks and starts clawing at me.

"Let me go! Let me go!" I have to grab her fists to keep her from punching me in the head, but she's too weak to land a good punch anyway.

"It's okay," I say. "You're safe and I'm not going to hurt you. I'm a friend. My name is Omaha, and I saved you from the WUG this morning. They had you in some kind of cage in the back of a transport. I couldn't leave you there, so I took you with me."

She stops struggling and tries to get a better look at me, but my headlamp is aimed at her and in the dark she can't see my face. I cautiously let go of her hands and give her the headlamp. She shines it in my face and I try not to wince.

"I don't remember," she says in a whisper, putting the light down.

"You were unconscious, but you're awake now and that's great," I babble. "Would you like to drink some water and eat some food?"

She accepts the canteen and greedily gulps down most of it. All the while her eyes never leave mine.

"Take it easy," I say with a sympathetic smile. "Just a little at a time so you don't get sick. Have a few bites of deer jerky. I made it myself."

Until now, I've been thinking about this girl as unwanted baggage, but as she chews the jerky and tries to make sense of where she is, I feel curious about her. I have never seen anyone with such striking features. She is absolutely beautiful, but in a totally different way than London.

"Is your name Nalim?" I ask.

Her eyes immediately grow suspicious. "Who told you that?"

I hold up the hand-held scanner and point to the UPC code on her arm. "I took this from the WUG vehicle too. I thought it might be useful."

Nalim's eyes widen as if she's suddenly remembered something.

"Oh no!" she says. "They can track me!" The look in her eyes changes to panic.

"We're deep in the woods. They can't find you here," I assure her.

"They can! They put this tracker implant in my arm." She points to the pea-sized bump above the UPC code.

Adrenaline pumps through my body. There is no doubt in my mind that the WUG are on their way here right now, right this minute. The urge to leave her and take off on my own is strong, but I know I can't do that.

"Close your eyes and look away," I tell her urgently. "This will hurt, but we have to get that out of your arm."

"Don't touch me!" She pulls away.

"Listen," I say, trying not to panic, "if the WUG find you, it will be very bad. Those soldiers who were transporting you are dead. I killed them. I know you don't know me. I don't know you either, but we both don't want anything to do with the WUG, so that makes us on the same side."

She exhales sharply and holds out her arm. I grab for my bug-out bag and pull out Grandpa's razor-sharp Boy Scout pocket knife. I am so anxious that my hand shakes a little. I take a calming breath and then another, and I pinch the pea-sized bump. It's hard as a rock. Without hesitating, I make a small incision, ignoring her gasp of pain, and then I squeeze the tracking device through the hole and put it in my pocket. I smear on some antibiotic cream from the German first aid kit and quickly bandage her arm.

"We have to move – now!" I say, jumping up to pull down the tarp and repack my gear.

She struggles to stand and I remember how weak she is. I could scream with frustration. London is counting on me, and here I've gotten myself tangled up with a WUG fugitive. Oh well, I think as I untie an end of the tarp, what's done is done.

The thwack thwack of a helicopter in the distance warns me that they're coming, and then the closer sound of dogs barking.

They are coming from the road from where we left the bike.

"Follow me!" I take Nalim's hand and pull her to her feet, abandoning the tarp and slinging my bag over my shoulder.

"Try to keep up," I whisper as we stumble down the hill toward the racing water of a creek.

There are flashlights behind us now and the dog barks are getting louder. The helicopter is nearly overhead, its spotlight shining down, looking to catch us in the beam. We stay under cover of trees and move steadily toward the stream. I have to give Nalim credit – she's staying on her own feet and barely stumbles. Fear must be giving her energy, too. It takes us just a few minutes to reach the stream, which rushes with water from hard spring rains. Thank God the moon is bright and I don't have to use my headlamp to see. My hands moving lightning fast, I break off a dead willow branch and twist the tip of my knife blade on the end to create a small hole, where I place the tracker implant that I cut from Nalim's arm moments earlier. I quickly peel a strip of willow bark from another branch and tie it around the dead stick to hold the tracker implant in place, and then I hurl the stick into the fastest part of the river. It surges downstream and vanishes into the darkness.

"Hopefully that will throw them off course long enough for us to escape," I whisper to her. "We have to go upstream. The dogs will be following our scent."

During our brief stop, all her energy drained away and now she stumbles and struggles to keep up. After only a minute I am dragging her along through the shallow part of the current while we hear the dogs barking with excitement as they start down the hill toward the stream.

"Come on come on come on," I say to myself, but it's no use. The girl is just too weak.

"I can't do it," she gasps, sitting down in the water. "Go! You don't have to get caught. Run and save yourself!"

She's giving me permission to go, and I've been thinking all day that I should never have gotten myself involved with this girl. But suddenly I don't want to leave her behind. A scout is loyal. I decide the WUG can't have her.

"Put your arms around my neck," I tell her, lifting her into my arms. I grunt with pain from my gunshot wound, but she feels even lighter than my bug-out bag. I put one foot in front of the other and start trudging upstream through the water to confuse the dogs. The flashlights are flickering through the trees and I can see they are almost to the water's edge. They are too close.

I turn a bend in the stream and duck under a large exposed tree root and put Nalim down on the sandy shore. I pull the German .22 revolver from my belt and crouch down. At least I can use it to stop the dogs from mauling us to death. The soldiers are at the stream's edge now. I can hear them talking on the radio to the helicopter. A beam of light shines just past me around the bend and then disappears in the opposite direction. I point the revolver toward the bend, ready to fire at the first sight of movement, either animal or human. My arm trembles with fear and I can't control my nerves.

"Brave...fearless" I whisper, trying to convince myself.

I hold the gun for what seems like an eternity, but no one comes around the bend. After a few moments I realize the dog barks are heading downstream. I breathe a deep sigh of relief and stick the revolver in my belt.

"They're following the tracking device downstream," I whisper. "I can't believe it worked."

She offers no response and I realize she's passed out again.

Carrying her up the hill without her holding on to me is hard work, especially with my damaged arm. The action has broken the wound back open. It feels like it takes forever to get back to the forest edge near the road where our bike is stashed. I can see the WUG vehicles parked fifty yards away. The lights are off and there doesn't seem to be any sign of activity. I use my binoculars to make sure and confirm the coast is clear then make my way to the bike. It's still there, covered with grass just like I left it.

I lay Nalim on the ground and look at her. She said I could leave her behind. It wouldn't be like abandoning her. Hadn't I saved her twice, at great risk to my own mission and myself? Surviving means making hard choices, and traveling with an unconscious girl who is a WUG fugitive is a risk I can't afford. With cold-blooded logic, I assess that she is of no use to me and will not improve my chances of survival or success in rescuing London.

But then I think about what I would have to tell Mom and Macy. They would look at me like I was some kind of monster, leaving her here for the WUG. And they would be right.

So just like that, I make my decision. I pick her up and put her on the bike, tying her to me with the overcoat again. I hate to do it, but I have to break the night silence with the high-pitched whine of the two-stroke motor. Under the light of the moon, I tear past the WUG vehicles toward Philadelphia. I smile a little imagining the soldiers and helicopter chasing a willow branch downstream. The thought crosses my mind to stop and glean more resources from their trucks, but distance is the best advantage I can gain right now.

I travel east for about three hours until I am completely overwhelmed by exhaustion. It's still pitch black, but I have to pull off and get some rest. I'm in the middle of farming country now and rarely see a homestead. I pass an old, dilapidated barn at the edge of a huge hay field and decide this is the best place to hole up for the rest of the night. I turn up the gravel driveway, cut off the engine and coast inside through the slightly open front door. There are hundreds of square bales of hay stacked in nice, neat piles from last fall. I can barely lift Nalim off the bike because my arms are so fatigued. I manage to get her onto a pile of loose hay and then I stumble over my own feet while I tuck the bike in a corner behind a big stack of bales. With the last of my strength, I pull out a few bales from the center of a big stack, creating a hole in the middle that is the perfect size for the both of us. I'm thirsty, but our canteen is almost empty and Nalim will need it more. I place it next to her just in case she wakes up while I'm sleeping.

Tonight, I close my eyes thinking about Mom and Macy. They have no idea how close to death I've come, twice already, and it's only been one day. This trip is not going at all as I had planned.

***

I awake to the sound of birds chirping and slits of rose-colored sunshine cutting across my body from cracks between the planks on the east wall. My exhaustion has gotten the best of me. The sun is already up and I'm angry with myself for sleeping so late. I push myself up from my hay bed, noting the soreness and heat in my wounded arm.

Red in the morning, sailor takes warning. Rain isn't too far away. I turn to check on Nalim, but there's no sign of her. My bug-out bag has been opened and several items are strewn about on the bale of hay beside me: empty food ration wrappers from the German MREs, my camo poncho, the photograph of

London, Mom's loaf of bread with a few pieces gone and the jar of poison monkshood jelly in the grape jelly jar.

"Oh no," I gasp under my breath.

She's eaten some of my munti poison. I never thought she would go through my pack. Why didn't I hide it? Why didn't I tell her not to eat it? Where has she gone? After everything I've done, has she robbed me and left? Horrible thoughts race through my mind.

Suddenly, a moving shadow catches my eye from outside the barn. I climb out of my hay bale shelter and peek around the edge of the door. It's Nalim. My first thought is that I'm glad to see she hasn't died from poison or stolen my stuff and run away, but as I watch her, I can't figure out what she's doing. It looks as if she is…well…dancing. She's walking back and forth in circles and throwing her feet around right in the middle of the tall alfalfa grass. It's the oddest thing I've ever seen, but I'm distracted by how beautiful she looks with the sun shining from behind her. Her blonde hair is glistening like golden Christmas tinsel and she looks nothing short of radiant, even in her tattered WUG prisoner outfit.

The meadow reminds me of home. London. A sense of dread and urgency makes me groan with frustration. Every minute I'm not getting closer to Philadelphia is another minute that she is in mortal danger.

A voice shakes me from my dire thoughts. "It's Omaha, right? I didn't hallucinate that?"

I can't see her face because I'm looking into the sun. "Yeah. I'm Omaha."

"I helped myself to some of your food."

"I noticed," I say. "Just as long as you didn't eat the grape jelly —" I start to tell her why, but she snaps at me.

"Don't worry; I didn't eat any of your precious grape jelly."

"Good," I growl impatiently, "because it's not food; it's poison. I dipped two arrows in it and killed the two WUG soldiers who had you. If you had helped yourself to my 'precious grape jelly,' you'd have vomited up purple bile and died in about forty seconds!" I realize I'm yelling. "And what the heck are you doing out here dancing around when the WUG soldiers might come driving down that road looking for you?"

"I'm not dancing," she replies calmly. "I'm gathering water. Are you thirsty?"

I was. Very thirsty, I realized, which was probably adding to my general crankiness. "There's no water out there." I'm thinking she maybe got hit on the head a little too hard.

"You're wrong," she says, walking toward me. I can't help but notice the German .22 revolver tucked into her waist—something else she helped herself to when she went through my pack. I see she has also tied two of my shirts around her chest and waist and two of my bandannas around her legs. I'm about to say something about it when she pulls loose a bandanna and shows it to me.

"It's dew, Omaha. I'm not dancing; I'm gathering dew. Open up."

I open wide and tilt my head back as she wrings a mouthful of fresh, cool dew water from the soaked bandanna.

"I already filled the canteen," she says, holding it out to me. I'm speechless for a moment.

"Well, um, that's creative." I'm genuinely surprised. "You might not just be dead weight to haul around after all."

"Speaking of that," she replies, ignoring my rudeness. "What happened last night? The last thing I remember was you dragging me into that ice-cold water."

"I was saving your life," I bristle. "The WUG followed your tracker downstream. After you passed out, I had to carry you through the forest, and then hold you on the bike for three hours until I found this barn. And in the meantime, I'm sure they've found the tracker implant in the willow stick, so we can assume the WUG are still looking for you."

She must see the look of resentment on my face, which I admit I'm not doing a very good job of hiding.

"Hey, I didn't ask you to take me!" she snaps. "What do you want from me, anyway?"

"I don't want anything from you. I don't even know you!"

"Where I'm from, people don't help strangers without expecting something in return," she says, her eyes narrowing as she sizes me up. "Everyone wants something. What do you want, Omaha?"

There is something ominous in her voice and I can feel my own anger rising. I take a swig from the canteen and calm down. I remind myself that she managed to fill our canteen. This is a good thing. If we're going to survive, we need to be a team. We shouldn't fight. A feeling of shame comes over me for how I've been acting. It was my decision to bring her along. She didn't ask me to, so I need to stop blaming her for my frustration that I'm not in Philadelphia already. I don't know how to say all this to the strange, beautiful girl.

"You planning on shooting someone with that pistol," I say instead, pointing to the revolver at her waist.

"If I have to," she says, her eyes hard. "I'm being chased by the WUG. And, I don't know who you are or what you want from me."

We stare at each other for a moment. I wish I knew what to say to make her trust me. Just as the moment is getting beyond awkward, a rabbit darts out of the tall grass and cuts across the gravel driveway to a new hiding place about thirty yards away. My eyes track it.

"Don't move," I say quietly as I creep back into the barn.

Within seconds I'm back with my slingshot loaded with an undipped munti. I can barely make out the shape of the rabbit's head through the tuft of grass where it stopped, but it's enough. I take five silent steps to get a better angle, draw my munti and land a perfectly humane headshot. The rabbit dies on impact.

"That was amazing!" Nalim looks at me with respect. "I've never seen a slingshot that shoots little arrows before." She examines the rabbit and then pulls out the munti and looks at it up close. "Did you carve this?"

"Yes, my dad showed me how. He brought the slingshot back from Asia. He got it off a Gi-Nong warrior." I'm aware that I'm babbling, so I focus on field dressing the rabbit while she continues to inspect the munti.

"Hungry?" I ask.

"I'm starved," she answers truthfully. And then I'm really seeing her – the dark shadows under her eyes; the stark bones of her face where there should be flesh. I remember the bruises I saw on her arms and legs. The girl has been starved, beaten, caged and probably drugged. I feel ashamed of myself for having been such a jerk to her. As she shoots me a curious look I can't help but notice how the bright morning sun makes her blue eyes shine like sapphires.

I use my machete to split up an old chunk of wood and clear the loose hay from a spot on the dirt floor to make a safe area to start a fire inside the barn. One spark from my fire striker into a petroleum jelly cotton ball gets a good hot fire going in no time. I hang the rabbit to cook over the fire on a scrap piece of barbed wire. While Nalim collects more dew water, I gather a fresh salad of greens from the edge of the alfalfa field that includes dandelion, plantain, shepherd's purse, red clover blooms, violet leaves and lambs quarter. I pile these on an old wooden plank and turn my attention back to Nalim, who is now babysitting the rabbit.

"So what's your story?" I ask. "So far, all I know is that you're a fugitive captured by the WUG and I found you half-dead in the back of a transport."

"I don't remember how I got there," she tells me, staring at the fire. "The last thing I remember before waking up next to you in the woods is getting smashed in the head by the butt of a WUG soldier's gun during an interrogation."

"So why were you being questioned?"

"It's a long story," she says, clearly not willing to discuss it. "I wouldn't give them what they wanted so they started beating me and that's the last thing I remember. How about you? What's your story?"

She's changing the subject and I bite back my irritation. I've risked my life to save hers– twice already–and she still doesn't trust me. Well maybe I'm the one who shouldn't trust her. She's the fugitive, not me.

"I'm headed east to find my friends and get them back home," I say tersely.

Nalim and I sit in silence, mesmerized by the delicious smell of roasting wild rabbit and conscious that both of us are holding back information. The sizzle of grease drippings reminds me how hungry I am. I tear off a nicely cooked piece of rabbit leg and hand it over to her. Then I tear one for myself and bite into the hot meat.

"Where are you from, anyway?" I ask, while at the exact

same moment, Nalim asks me, "So where are these friends of yours?"

In unison we both answer: "Philadelphia."

Chapter Six

"You're going to Philadelphia?" Nalim's face is flushed with enthusiasm. "That's where I'm from! My dad doesn't know where I am. He probably thinks I'm dead. We're not that far are we? How long will it take us to get there if we leave right now?"

I realize she has no idea that Philadelphia has been scheduled for destruction. I break the news to her and she drops her head into her hands in despair. I'm trying to think of what I can say to comfort her when she looks up at me suddenly.

"Have they started the bombings yet?"

"I don't know," I say. "But they will soon. We have two days, at most."

Her pale face looks ashen, but she swallows bravely. "He might have escaped. Dad had boats stashed at the river on the south side of the city. It was part of his get-away plan if things got really bad. I'll go with you that far and then I'll head downstream to New Jersey from there to see if I can catch up with him." She stands, impatient to be off. We finally agree on something: we need to hurry.

But we're going to need food for the journey. Using my pocket knife, I quickly shred the cooked rabbit meat and assemble two pulled rabbit sandwiches with Mom's bread and the wild greens I gathered.

"Here," I say while holding one of the sandwiches toward Nalim. "Eat this. We need to get on the road." She takes it gratefully and eats it as fast as I eat mine. Like most wild animals, the rabbit tastes faintly of what it eats. A diet of red clover, lush alfalfa and tart yellow wood sorrel gives the meat a sweet, nutty flavor. The fire adds a light smoky flavor that makes this rabbit one of the best I've ever eaten. Nalim murmurs her approval as she swallows the last bite.

I start to pack my bug-out bag, and as she hands me back my shirts and bandannas I can tell Nalim has something on her mind.

"What?" I ask.

"I'm sorry I've held you back," she says frankly. "You'd probably be there already if it wasn't for me."

"Yeah, I probably would be," I say, trying not to sound as bitter as I feel. "The past twenty-four hours certainly wasn't a part of my plan."

"I get it, okay? I'm a huge inconvenience. I already feel bad about it," she snaps. "You don't have to make me feel worse. I was trying to be nice."

I am reminded of why I don't like being around people. I'm not good at expressing myself. London always knew what I was trying to say. I never say the wrong things around her, not the way I keep doing with Nalim.

"Well, um, I sure would be thirsty right now if it wasn't for you." I take a big gulp of water from the dew-filled canteen.

She rolls her eyes, but I can tell things are okay between us, at least for now. Dad always told me that your gut would tell you within the first thirty seconds whether or not you can trust someone. I realize that I trust Nalim, even though I know she's not telling me everything.

We are packed and on the road in minutes. It's seven thirty in the morning, which I consider a late start, but at least we're on the road. My arm throbs in pain with the vibration of the dirt bike, but the ride is much more comfortable with Nalim behind me instead of tied onto my lap. I stop to consult the map a few times and am pleased to see that even though we have to take smaller back roads than I'd planned, we're making pretty good time. I'm worried about running into more WUG, but I'm also enjoying the sun on my face as we cruise down remote farm roads. I tense every time we pass a farmer in a pick-up truck, but Nalim just gives a cheerful wave as if there's nothing odd about us being here. Everyone waves back.

The road we're on takes us past a prosperous-looking horse farm. The white picket fences seem to stretch for miles. I'm so enamored by the beautiful pastures I barely notice how close we are to the main farmhouse. It's set back just off the road about two hundred yards ahead.

"I'd sure love to live there," Nalim shouts in my ear.

"Me too! This farm is beautiful," I reply into the wind.

I slow the bike down so that we can see every detail of the house as we pass. There is a vineyard out back next to the biggest garden I've ever seen. The chicken coop is more like a chicken condominium and four baby lambs are playing in the pasture. As we get closer to the house, I notice something that just doesn't look right. A man is lying across the front porch steps. I've never seen someone lie across steps like that. And then, above the whine of the bike's engine, I hear a scream.

"Something is strange here," Nalim says. I agree.

We are now right out in front of the house, a stone's throw from the porch. I'm driving so slow it's hard to keep the bike upright. Through the kitchen window I can see a woman fighting with a man and I can hear a girl screaming from somewhere else in the house.

"Omaha, look!" Nalim points to the back of the house. "A WUG truck!"

I see it parked in the back yard. A knot forms in my stomach as I cut the engine and coast behind a big stand of pine trees on the far side of the yard. I can't get those screams out of my head. Mom and Macy are home alone right now. What if this was our house? What if those women inside that house were Mom and Macy? I lightly pound my head against the handlebars of the bike in frustration. I can't afford any more delays, but I'll never forgive myself if I keep driving. My mind is telling me one thing and my gut another. Every moment I spend trying to help other people is a moment that London may not survive in Philadelphia. But my scouting training is stronger. I can be of service here. I need to try.

Nalim jumps off the bike and double checks that the .22 revolver, which she has kept with her, is full of rounds. She's clearly made up her mind already so the decision is out of my hands. I grab my slingshot, efficiently dip five munti in monkshood jelly and stash my pack under one of the large pines.

"Right," says Nalim in a very confident tone. "What's the plan?"

I'm really surprised at her eagerness to wage battle against WUG soldiers after she's been their prisoner. And she certainly seems comfortable with the revolver. I watch as she tears a strip of fabric from the hem of her shirt and ties her hair back away from her face.

"Let's try to get in and out of here as fast as possible," I reply. "You stay outside and keep watch. Yell if you need me." She glances at my slingshot and then meets my eyes and nods once.

As I approach the front porch, Nalim stays tight to the house and disappears around the back corner. It's clear the man on the steps has been shot and killed. I suspect he used to live here. I step over his body and slip through the slightly ajar front door. My moccasins are dead silent. I can hear the struggle and muffled screams from the next room and also from upstairs. I load a munti and peek around the doorway to engage my enemy. His back is to me. He is wearing the same olive-colored uniform as the WUG soldiers I killed yesterday. I take in the details of the scene while my pulse races with adrenaline. He has torn the flower-print dress of a woman that appears to be about my mom's age, and he's fumbling with his belt. I sight my kill shot and step through the doorway into the room as I send a deadly munti directly into the base of his skull.

The soldier reels with pain and surprise. He has the presence of mind to spin around and fire his compact automatic rifle. Bullets spray the wall behind me as I dive and roll through the doorway into the hallway. I hear him hit the floor and know it won't be long until he's dead. I immediately hear heavy steps running down the hallway upstairs. I reach into my pocket to reload my slingshot, but nothing is there. Frantically, I look around and see munti scattered across the floor. Everything seems to happen in slow motion. I hear the action of a gun chambering a round for battle as heavy boots move cautiously down the stairs. I leap to my feet, step around the corner of the staircase and silently pull Grandpa's machete from the sheath. I will need the steadiness of that oak and the force of that lighting now more than ever. My pulse is pounding against the solid oak handle. I take a deep breath to steady my nerves, and then I raise the machete over my shoulder and position my legs to strike.

I can't see who is coming down the stairs, but from the vibrations of his tread I can tell he's a much larger man than me, but smaller than the last elk I hunted and killed with Grandpa. My senses are tuned way up, just as they are when I'm hunting. I hear his labored breathing and smell the stale stench of cigarette smoke. The woman in the next room is sobbing and her daughter upstairs calls for her mother. I hear the death throes of the poisoned soldier in the kitchen. A bird chirps outside on the porch and a bead of sweat runs down my back.

The soldier reaches the downstairs hallway and turns right into the kitchen to see what happened to his friend. With his back turned, he doesn't see me coming. I stomp his right knee inward with every ounce of force I can muster. Up close, he is a huge man, at least twice my size, and through my moccasins I can feel his knee come apart and buckle in a direction it was never intended to bend. The bone splits through his pants on the other side as he bellows in pain and crumples to the floor.

"Take a man's knees and you take the man," Dad told me more than once when he was teaching me hand-to-hand combat techniques.

Bullets fire randomly from the automatic rifle in his hands and I hope the woman has fled, but I can't spare her a glance. I'm crouched over him, poised for my final blow. A force of lightning thrusts my machete through the center of his back. Blood sprays my hand and face as the air in his lungs escapes around the old lawnmower blade that is my weapon. His labored breathing changes to a low gurgle and I know from hunting large game that a blow to the chest like this only takes a few seconds to end it.

I look up as the woman in the flower print dress stares at me in horror.

"It's okay," I say. "I'm not going to hurt you."

She runs past me and up the stairs to check on her daughter.

Three gunshots ring out from behind the house. I remember Nalim is still out there. I tear through the kitchen and burst through the back door to find her standing over a dead German shepherd wearing a WUG collar.

She gasps when she sees me, but I reassure her that it's not my blood. I stare at my hands. It all happened so fast. It's ten in the morning and I've killed two WUG soldiers. It took me ninety seconds to kill the two men. Ninety seconds ago, they were alive and now they're dead. I bend down and wipe the blood off my machete in the clean grass. There is a hose nearby and I vigorously wash my hands and face, but I still feel dirty. I go back inside and collect my munti and then I methodically repack my slingshot and put my machete back in its sheath. These familiar acts steady me.

I wasn't fearless, Grandpa, but I got the job done, I think to myself.

"Omaha? Are you okay?" Nalim is touching my arm. She looks worried.

"Yeah. Let's deal with the bodies and the truck and then get out of here."

"I think there's someone in the truck – a prisoner."

"Alive?"

"Maybe."

We walk over to the truck and I open the back door to find a middle-aged man bound and gagged in the back seat. I untie the gag and help him sit up. He smells rancid, like he's been rolled in old garbage. The stink makes me feel sick.

"Cut these ropes before they get back here," he says, holding his wrists toward me with a smile that unsettles me. He has a UPC code on his wrist. As I untie him, I feel his wrist. There is no pea-sized lump above it like there was on Nalim.

"They aren't coming back," I tell him as I slice the ropes that bind his ankles. "What's your name?"

"Just call me Fink," he says.

I watch as he looks Nalim up and down with a hungry expression and I immediately don't trust this man. He has a large scar that stretches from his left eye down to his neck. His hair is long, greasy and unkempt. He's wearing a work camp uniform that is dark gray from dirt and ragged on every edge. Before I can stop him he dives into the front seat and grabs a pistol from the glove box. He expertly checks to see that it's loaded and then he laughs – it is not a nice laugh – and waves it in the air. He reaches under the seat and pulls out a full bottle of whiskey, cracks it open and takes a big swig.

"Ahh, just what Fink needs," he says. He looks over at Nalim and leers.

The two women from inside the house appear at the back door. The girl has been beaten up pretty badly.

"Fink's day just keeps getting better and better!" Fink springs out of the truck and points his gun at the women. "Three girls and two guys: Fink likes these odds."

I make eye contact with Nalim. We're in trouble.

"Fink, help me get the dead soldiers into the truck," I say. "As soon as the WUG realizes they're not reporting to command they'll send a squad to check. I saw an abandoned mining quarry a few miles back. We can dump the truck there and then be on our way."

"There's another quarry, and bigger, about two miles up," says the woman, backing up toward the door of her house. She has pushed her daughter inside and out of sight. "It's set off the road a bit. No one's ever there."

"Fink's not going anywhere," Fink says with a smile. "Fink is staying right here with his new family."

I have to think quickly. I'm not leaving him here with these two women.

"Sure," I say. "You can stay here if you want. Be sure to give the WUG and their dogs our best. They should be here within the hour. We'll be down the road at the safe house. They slaughtered a pig this morning. Going to have a barbeque, with lots of beer and women and probably a good poker game going. But you stay here and shoot it out with the WUG."

Fink pauses and stares me straight in the eye. "Safe house, eh?"

"That's what I said."

"If you're lying, boy, Fink will kill you with his own two hands."

"It's the truth," says Nalim. "What are we waiting around for? The faster we get out of here the faster we get to the party." She gives him a slow smile that promises fun. Fink takes another swig and offers her the bottle. Nalim considers it and then accepts it and takes a big gulp and hands it back. Fink is grinning in a way that makes my skin crawl. He gestures with his gun toward the truck.

"Let's get this party started!"

I keep an eye on Fink while the woman and girl find two big sheets. The whole time, Fink and Nalim pass the bottle back and forth. I'm worried about how alcohol will affect her, but Nalim looks much different from the girl I found in the truck. I get the feeling that Nalim is no stranger to confrontation and can handle herself just fine. The German .22 is out of sight, but I trust that she can get to it if she needs to.

Fink and I load the two dead WUG soldiers into the back of the military truck while Nalim stores my bike in the barn of the grateful women. I doubt I'll ever be back to get it, but I'd rather keep it here than ditch it in the woods. Maybe these women can use it.

Fink answers a call of nature with his gun trained on me, but I still manage to scribble a quick note to Mom and Macy and ask the woman to mail it for me. Fink is watching, but when she takes it she slips me a Hershey bar. I almost try to give it back but I realize Fink will just steal it, so I tuck it into my pocket. Today is Nalim's birthday. It will be a nice surprise for her later.

Nalim comes back outside wearing different clothes. Her WUG work camp uniform was mostly rags, and she looks startlingly normal now wearing faded blue jeans, a fitted black t-shirt and brown leather boots. She has an olive canvas jacket tied around her waist, and I think I can see the German .22 tucked underneath. I feel a wash of relief at that.

Seeing her in regular clothes, I'm struck again by how beautiful she is. Unfortunately, Fink notices, too.

"You clean up nice! Fink likes!" He hands her the bottle again and she shakes her head, but with a smile.

"Later for me. But thanks!" She's flirting with him and he

likes it.

"Time to go," I say with fake enthusiasm. "Let's find that party!"

Fink insists on riding in the back seat. I can feel his gun aimed at my head, but I concentrate on keeping the big, heavy, military vehicle on the road. The smell of whiskey from the back seat makes me wary. It was a full bottle when he started drinking but it's now about half full. I'm guessing Fink is an angry drunk.

We find the quarry up the road in a few minutes. It's a perfect spot to sink the truck with the bodies. We watch it get swallowed into the black water and then Fink swears and yells and dances around. The gun is still in his hand, still trained loosely on me.

According to the scale on my map, the south side of Philadelphia is just thirty-seven miles from the quarry. We're so close, but it feels like it's a continent away. I'm burning with frustration at all the time we're wasting. First we have to deal with the Fink problem. Then we'll have to avoid getting captured by WUG patrols, which will be everywhere the closer we get to the city. Even traveling cross-country through fields and forest, we'll have to move carefully. My rap sheet has grown quite a bit in three days. I've killed four WUG soldiers, looted WUG property, sunk a WUG truck and now I'm aiding and abetting two WUG fugitives. How much better can it get?

"Where's the party, boy?" Fink slurs his words, but the gun is steady in his hands and it's still pointed at me.

"It's close. Just down this trail," I say calmly, adjusting my bug-out bag on my shoulder. "I saw that pig they slaughtered this morning. It was a nice, fat one. Come on!"

Nalim and I start walking away from him as if we're

perfectly confident. I'm tensed for the gunshot to my back, but I hear him swear and start to follow.

"That was a good thing you did back there, Omaha," Nalim says quietly as we trudge east on a deer trail. We have to pretend everything is normal and that there isn't a drunk, armed psychopath behind us expecting a barbeque in a few hundred yards.

"Anyone would have done it," I say with a shrug. "That could have been my mom and sister. I'd hope someone would help them in a situation like that if I wasn't around."

"And you didn't ask them for anything in return for helping them?" She gives me a curious look.

"I'm a Boy Scout. We do the right thing because it's the right thing to do. End of story." I shoot her a look. "Did you ask them for anything?"

She blushes and I realize the clothes she's wearing weren't a gift; they were payment. My disappointment shows on my face.

"They offered. I didn't take anything," she says defensively. "Where I'm from, people only help you if there's something in it for them. Not everyone can afford to be a Boy Scout."

She says it teasing, but I hear sadness in her voice, too, and when I look up she's giving me a frank look of admiration. I get the funniest feeling, like little butterflies in my stomach.

"Omaha," Nalim says too softly for Fink to hear, "the gun…" She is reaching for it slowly under the jacket.

"Stop right there!" Fink bellows. I can feel suspicion rolling off him like stink. The whiskey bottle is empty.

"We're nearly there," I say, pointing in front of us. "You'll see the house any minute now."

"Enough talking. I don't think so. Fink is done walking. We start the party right here." I hear the familiar click of a revolver's hammer. I have never been in more danger in my life than I am at this moment.

"Throw your little gun here, missy, real easy now. You don't want your little friend to accidentally get shot through the head, now do you?"

Nalim scowls and tosses it at his feet. He scoops it up with the other hand, now aiming one gun at me and one gun at her.

"And that big knife," he says to me.

I hesitate.

"Fink'll put a bullet in yer head, boy," he says, and I have absolutely no doubt that he will. After all, there are no consequences.

I draw my machete and toss it point first into the ground between his feet.

"Now what's in that fancy pack of yours, boy?" Fink demands. "What are you hiding from Fink? Toss it here, slow and easy. You do anything stupid and I'll shoot her in the leg. I can still have my fun with her and we can both watch her bleed out before I shoot your face off."

I shrug off my pack and throw it to him. He shoves Nalim's pistol in his pants and shakes out the contents of my bag. The photo of London falls to the ground.

"What's this?" he says looking up at me.

"Leave it alone," I say sharply.

"Oh, it seems he's two-timing you, missy," he says to Nalim. He looks back at me with a lewd wink. "Don't worry boy, Fink approves!"

He draws his tongue across the back of the picture and then sticks it to his greasy forehead.

"Don't you worry about her, boy. Fink will find her and take real good care of her."

I will kill him.

He gives a nasty laugh and holds up my slingshot. "Ain't that cute! You could kill yourself a mousey with that thing!" He flings it into the woods as I grit my teeth, and then he finds something to make him genuinely happy. Fink holds up my mom's jar of pickled eggs.

"Are you hiding food from Fink, boy?"

He throws the lid aside and crams two eggs in his mouth. White pieces of egg fall down his face and sprinkle the mud below as he chews them up. It's grotesque to watch. He points the gun at Nalim now.

"Don't think about doing anything stupid, boy," he warns. "One in the leg is all it will take, and there will be all that pretty red blood and her pretty, pretty screams."

He washes down the mouthful of egg with a sloppy gulp of water from the canteen.

He digs deeper into the pile of my gear and pulls out the remaining bread slices, the bag of dried apples and the jar of grape jelly. Nalim and I look at each other, thinking the same thing. Fink continues to shove random bites of food into his mouth. He doesn't seem interested in the grape jelly.

"Leave the grape jelly alone!" blurts Nalim. "You have to leave something for us."

"Oh, Fink'll have plenty for you later, missy, don't you worry." He makes a lewd gesture and I want to strangle him so badly.

"The jelly's mine. You can't have it," I say.

"Fink can have whatever he wants, boy." He twists off the lid with his mouth and smashes the last slice of bread down into the jelly.

"Fink likes toast and jelly," he says just before thrusting the purple dripping bread slice into his mouth.

He makes a contorted face and spits the mouthful of food right out.

"That is vile!" gasps Fink. He tosses the jar to the side. It lands haphazardly against a nearby log, thankfully unbroken. He spits a few times and takes a swig from the canteen to clean out his mouth.

"Time for dessert," says Fink with a new, menacing tone in his voice. He aims the gun at my head and I can't help but notice how steady that arm is, despite all the whiskey he's had. He gestures to Nalim. "Come to Fink now."

Nalim gives me a panicked look. My heart is pounding with tension. If he didn't have the gun, I would strangle him with my bare hands.

"Fink'll shoot the boy if you don't get over here right now. I've waited long enough."

I can't believe the monskhood poison isn't working. It was rotten luck that Fink never swallowed it so it's not in his bloodstream. I frantically scan the ground around me for anything I can use as a weapon. There isn't even a good-sized rock I can use to bash in his head. Nalim is only a few steps away from him now, and Fink still has the gun aimed at me.

Suddenly, his face winches with pain and he makes a choked, gurgling noise. Nalim and I freeze as he gives us warning looks. He still has the gun, but now he's clawing his stomach in an attempt to stop whatever is groaning and heaving inside of him.

He buckles in half and screams, "What have you done—"

His words are staunched by an eruption of purple foam and liquor and egg pieces spewing from his mouth and nose. The whites of his eyes turn a deep maroon and a wet purple stain grows on the backside of his pants and down his legs. He keels over onto the ground and steaming purple bile runs out from under the hem of his pants. His body seizes and convulses for a few seconds and then there is silence.

Nalim vomits up her breakfast and the whiskey she drank. I come close to losing my breakfast, too. I have never seen any sight as disgusting as Fink. I help her sit down, and then I sink to the ground next to her. There are no words for what has just happened.

"Now I'm really glad I didn't eat that jelly this morning," she finally says. "Where in the world did you get that stuff?"

"It's an old family recipe. I've never seen someone eat it before and I hope I never have to again. That was awful!"

"He deserved it." Nalim gives a shudder and turns away.

I start repacking my bug-out bag, carefully avoiding the pools of purple vomit on the ground around it. I screw the top back on the grape jelly jar and tuck it safely into a side pocket. I walk a few yards into the woods and retrieve my slingshot. Then I remove the picture from Fink's forehead and wipe it clean on my pants.

Dnoces Tnemdnema, I say to London silently, wherever she is. If it's worth fighting for, it's worth dying for.

"Let's go," I say aloud to Nalim. "No more distractions. I have to get to Philadelphia."

CHAPTER SEVEN

Once we're rid of Fink we get a second wind of energy and move fast through the hilly countryside. I can't believe it's only 11 in the morning, with all that's happened. Three men dead and we're practically out of food. It feels like I ate that rabbit sandwich a week ago. I don't complain, because I'm sure it's harder for Nalim, and to her credit she doesn't complain, either. At least there's still a bag of jerky left. I share a few pieces with her. The protein gives us a little fuel to burn, and we set a brisk pace. I want to eat up the miles and get to London, but I stop a few times to gather handfuls of juicy mulberries that grow on low-hanging branches in the sun. The purple juice dribbles down our chins. The first chance I get, I rinse Fink's germs off the canteen and refill it from a seep in a small rock outcropping.

Unfortunately, my plan of keeping to the woods is becoming less and less realistic the closer we get to the city. In just a few miles, the terrain changes from farmland and forest to empty suburban developments. The stories I've heard on the subnet didn't prepare me for the miles and miles of desolate, overgrown subdivisions with abandoned houses, playgrounds, parks and strip malls. Ghost towns. Looters followed the work camp drafts and stole away anything of value and smashed up most of what they left behind. It looks like the aftermath of a tornado. But even the worst Mother Nature has to offer couldn't fill a place with such a feeling of complete despair and hopelessness. People did this to one another. It's ugly. The reality of what the WUG is doing to my country is ugly. Worse than I'd ever imagined. I avert my eyes from the hollow shells of homes that were once full of life, energy and dreams. "You haven't seen this before?" Nalim notices my bleak expression. "This is what all of America is going to look like, eventually. It's happening everywhere." I notice she doesn't call our country Unimerica.

"All these people—" I feel so helpless.

"Sentenced to work camps. Did you know they split up families? It's how they take away our hope, our reason to live. It's like this around all the big cities. We're now slaves for the entire world, Omaha, didn't you know that? Some of our people are sent abroad to work in factories, mines and worse."

"I had no idea it was this bad," I say quietly. I'd heard talk like this on the subnet, but I'd dismissed it as conspiracy theory. Looking around me now, I'm absolutely sure it's true.

"Where have you been the past two years, Boy Scout?" Nalim snorts derisively and this time the nickname doesn't sound so friendly. "Under a rock?"

I have been under a rock of sorts. I didn't want to know the truth about what was happening to people outside of my little bubble of home. Somewhere along the way, I guess I decided I could only care about Mom, Macy, London and Rake. It's amazing how much can happen when you're pretending it doesn't matter. In this moment I feel an overwhelming sense of duty to my country. But what can one person do in the face of an all-powerful enemy? I hate feeling helpless.

In Scouting, we focus on what we can do, and on getting it done. I remind myself of that. Just keep moving, Omaha. Get to London and then take the next step, and the next, until you can do your part to push the WUG back to where they came from.

"How do you know so much about the WUG?" I ask Nalim as we trudge down the empty street. Instead of answering she waves me over to one of the abandoned houses and points to a spigot on the side. I'm so thirsty my tongue feels twice its normal size in my mouth. I fill the canteen and hand it to her first, and we both drink our fill. Grandpa always said if you're hungry and have no food, fill your belly with water. The water definitely helps, but I wish Fink hadn't eaten Mom's pickled eggs. I could really go for one right now (I have to banish the grotesque image of Fink from my mind and hope the memory won't ruin pickled eggs for me forever).

"Five-minute break," Nalim says, collapsing on the overgrown grass with a groan.

I take the opportunity to slip through the shattered back patio door and into the abandoned house. It's completely ransacked and anything worth having is long gone. I rifle through the kitchen pantry and drawers, hoping to find something to eat, but nothing remains except empty food cans, wrappers and mouse droppings. The wild places have more to offer me on this journey. Luckily, I'm comfortable with that.

Back outside, I roll up my sleeve and unwind the bandage around the gunshot wound. There is a little yellow pus, which is worrisome. I wash it gingerly under the faucet and smear more antibiotic cream on it and wrap it in a fresh bandage. My med kit supplies are getting low, but I'm hoping I won't have any more need of it.

While Nalim rests, I pace around what used to be the backyard of this house, hoping to find remnants of a kitchen garden or fruit trees, but I all I find are dandelions. I pluck some greens and wash them under the spigot, and while I'm at it I stick my head under the running water and then shake off like a dog. I offer some of the greens to Nalim. We're both hungry enough to find them tasty, although they aren't usually a favorite of mine unless they're mixed into a salad with other greens or the roots are nicely roasted and ground into a coffee-like drink.

I'm balancing against a kid's swing set matted with honeysuckle and looking at the sky, which is growing overcast – I give it a fifty-fifty chance for actual rain – when Nalim sits up.

"So, that picture," she says, a little too casually, "who is she?"

I spit out some grit. "No one you need to know about."

"I'm just being friendly," she continues, ignoring my outburst. "She looks vaguely familiar, that's why I'm asking."

I shrug. "You ask a lot of questions, and you don't answer mine. Why do you know so much about the WUG? Why were they interrogating you?"

Nalim flops back down and folds her jacket into a pillow for her head. "Why do they interrogate anyone? They want information. They knew rebels were planning to strike in Philadelphia and they thought I knew something about it. So they grabbed me off the streets, sentenced me to the work camps, but made a detour to the interrogation center to torture me. Any more questions?"

"Yeah. Why you? Why did they think you'd know anything about rebels?"

"Because I openly defended a hungry woman against WUG soldiers in the streets. And they found out my dad is leader of the rebellion in Philadelphia."

I can't believe this! "Wait a minute. Your father started the revolt? Your father is the reason London is trapped in Philadelphia? And you're just now telling me this!?"

"London? That's in England." Nalim is confused. "How could it be trapped in Philadelphia? What are you talking about?"

I take out the photograph and wave it in her face. "This. Is. London! And it's your father's fault that she's going to be killed by the WUG! If he hadn't started the rebellion, she would have been home by now. It's his fault!"

I throw the canteen on the ground in a fit of rage. I want to scream with frustration. I've wasted all this time saving the daughter of the man who caused this mess! This is like a sick joke.

"Calm down!" Nalim slides the canteen out of my reach. "Do you really think the whole world revolves around Omaha? Honestly, you're crazy! Philadelphia wasn't quarantined when I was captured, I don't know what happened. You told me, remember?! There are bigger things going on here other than whether or not you're reunited with your little girlfriend."

"She's not my girlfriend!" I glare at her, even angrier now that she's made me admit this aloud. London is not my girlfriend, no matter how many times I've imagined that she is. We had one kiss, and it was to say goodbye. She never came home to visit. She never once wrote, "I miss you, Omaha." It was always, "I miss you, Macy and Mom."

"Okay, your friend, then." Nalim gives me a sympathetic look, which just makes me feel worse. "My point is you're mad at the wrong people. It's the WUG who are destroying Philadelphia right now. The rebels are fighting for everyone's freedom."

"You should have told me right away that you're a rebel."

"I didn't know if I could trust you." She squirms a little.

"Trust me?" I say bitterly. "I only saved your life – twice! I've been completely truthful with you. But go ahead; think what you want about me. I really don't care."

"You're taking this all wrong!" She glares at me. "Where I come from you can't trust anyone. A whole city will stand in the streets and watch the WUG punish starving women and children and not say anything!" Now she sounds bitter, too. "That's my reality, Omaha. While you've been hiding in your little forest playing Boy Scouts, the rest of us have been dealing with real life under WUG tyranny."

"There's nothing wrong with how I live," I say stubbornly, folding my arms. "Boy Scouts train for leadership, community service, teamwork, and being prepared." She rolls her eyes, and I shoot back, "It's because I'm a Boy Scout that I saved you from the WUG and took you with me, even though you slowed me down. Boy Scouts teach values, and I'm not ashamed of that."

"You're not the only one with values," she says, equally stubbornly, folding her arms and glaring right back at me. "But the rebellion puts freedom for all above our individual well-being. How long do you think you can hide your family from the WUG? They'll find you, too, one day, and do this—" she gestures to the empty houses around us— "to your home. Not even an Eagle Scout could be prepared enough to survive the

WUG invasion alone. The only way to stop them is to work together. This war is bigger than just you and me and your London. Don't you get that?"

I want to scream at her to shut up and leave me alone. I don't want to hear it. I don't want to hear that I won't have the happy ending of my fantasy, where I rescue London and we go back home and she is in love with me like I am with her, and our life goes back to the way it was before Grandpa died, before the WUG took over our country.

I can't face Nalim right now, so I pick up my pack and start walking. I hear her get up and follow a few steps behind. I'm too steamed to slow down. I estimate we have another 30 miles to go. We'll get there by tomorrow afternoon if we move fast. But now the whole journey feels like a fool's mission. How will I even find London when I get there? Is she with Rake? Are they still alive? Why am I risking my own life to find out?

I know the answer to that. It's London. I have no choice. A scout is loyal. Dnoces Tnemdnema. London is worth fighting for, and I would die for her if I had to. I just hope I don't have to and that she isn't dead already.

***

I stomp along, nursing my resentment for a while, aware of Nalim somewhere behind me. I'm thinking she can find her own way from now on; I'm done rescuing her. But then I hear her cry out. Alarmed, I spin around, my hand on my machete, but she's just tripped over a tree root. She picks herself up with a grim, determined look and I feel grudging respect for her. I've been taking my frustration and anger out on her, but I know this situation isn't her fault. I made my own choices, and I'm acting like a baby. She has been through a lot more than I have and she's not giving up. Despite all of our arguing, and her keeping vital information from me, I still do trust her.

There are two last pieces of jerky that I've been saving in case of an emergency. I give them both to Nalim as a peace offering. She hesitates, but she is too hungry to refuse. She mumbles, "Thanks," and starts devouring them.

"Do you really think there's a way to make things right again?" I ask after a mile or two of silently trudging side by side through overgrown grass and around broken concrete slabs.

"My dad does. He says there's a bigger plan to end WUG rule – not just in Unimerica, but also all over the world. We have allies. We're not alone in this, Omaha."

I couldn't help but notice how she said "we." Does she think I've joined her revolution? Because I haven't. Grandpa used to say, "Better to make your own path than to follow a lost cause."

She continues to tell me more details about the revolt in Philadelphia and about her dad's dreams of ending the WUG's rule. She talks about large underground rallies and meetings of like-minded people. She also tells me that some of our own have turned traitor. A former U.S. general is now commanding the WUG forces that are moving on east coast cities. I can't believe anyone could do that to his or her own people. It makes me sick.

"And then there are a lot of ex-military who aren't doing anything. They're just waiting for someone else to get rid of the WUG," she says darkly. My father spent months trying to recruit them to the rebellion, but a lot were too scared to join us. They said they have to look after their own first." She glares at me, and I know she's lumping me in with them. Is that fair? I want to get rid of the WUG so I can go back to living my life the way it was, but what good will fighting them do if the people I love are hurt in the process?

I know it's not fair to be angry with Nalim about this, but I still don't want to be a part of her rebellion, and it's not because I'm a coward. At least, I hope it's not. Mom and Macy count on me. I can't just run off and join the fight. But this journey has opened my eyes to the truth that focusing only on my family's survival is a short-term solution. Even if I save London and Rake and make it back home, what kind of future will we all have if the WUG still controls our nation? Suddenly, holing up in the bunker feels like giving up on America. We can't just hide and hope the invaders will go away. But the situation seems so hopeless, and I don't deal well with hopelessness. I need to focus on what I have control over, what I can do, like feeding my family and keeping them safe.

I can't fix this. Nalim is right and I know it: it might take the WUG a while to find us, but eventually our town will become another ghost town. The WUG have the most sophisticated technology ever developed by humans. They are ruthless and greedy, and they don't value human life or respect individual rights. How can anyone defeat them? It's impossible.

Now that Nalim has decided to trust me, she tells me more about herself as we walk. Her mother was killed during the first month of the WUG take-over of America when she tried to stop a soldier from hurting an old man on the street. "They laughed and put a bullet in her head," Nalim says. "Dad and I were inside, watching through the window. He had to hold me because I wanted to run outside to be with her. They would've shot me, too, and him. The WUG don't see us as people. We're cattle to them."

I guess I can understand why she and her dad are so deep into the rebellion. Maybe I would be too, if I saw the WUG murder Mom or Macy or London and there was nothing I could do to stop them.

"I was an idiot for blaming your father for putting London in danger." I've wanted to say that for the last few miles.

"I get it. You're worried about her. You must care a lot about London to risk everything to find her." There is curiosity in her tone, and invitation to say more, but I don't want to talk about London with her, for some reason.

"I do," is all I say. "She would do the same for me."

I say that, but I'm not sure she would. I hope she would, but we haven't seen each other in so long. Her feelings for me might have changed, even though mine haven't for her.

"Well she's lucky to have a friend like you" Nalim says, "and so am I, Boy Scout." She punches me lightly on my not-hurt arm and I blush a little.

I pull London's picture from my pocket and show it to Nalim again. "You said earlier that she looks familiar? Have you seen her?"

Nalim looks closely. "She does look familiar but I can't place her," she replies.

"It's an old photo anyway," I murmur to myself as I fold it back up and tuck it away.

All of this talking has caused us to slow down. I pick up the pace. London is waiting.

**

The closer we get to Philadelphia, the more carefully we have to travel because there are other people on the roads and trails. We pass dozens of refugees who must have escaped Philadelphia before the barricades went up. Some are walking, some are riding bikes and others are pushing shopping carts and pulling wagons with their scant belongings. Nalim and I are in agreement that we can't afford to trust anyone. We duck out of sight when we see someone approaching. The lost time eats at my gut. My sense of anxiety is building, and I know we're running out of time to save London.

We're moving as silently and swiftly as we can. It's somewhere around four o'clock in the afternoon, when I suddenly see the unmistakable neck of a giraffe moving through scrub brush up ahead.

"Nalim, look!!" I yell, pointing.

Nalim tries not to laugh at the expression on my face, but doesn't succeed, and soon we're both cracking up. When she catches her breath, she explains that animals from the Philadelphia Zoo were released by the WUG, who like to hunt them for sport. A few, like this giraffe, must have escaped the city. We see a second one towering over an abandoned strip mall in the distance. It's the oddest thing I've ever seen. Now that I know to listen for them, I hear monkey screeches and a strange braying that might be a zebra. I stop several times to examine scat that concerns me. The size of it tells me the animal is large, and the bits of bone and hair tell me it's a carnivore. I move a few munti into the outer pockets of my bug-out bag and keep the slingshot close. Be Prepared. We may not be at the top of the food chain in this upside-down rim of Philadelphia.

As the afternoon wears on, we speak less and I pay more attention to potential dangers. Dogs from the ghost towns have formed wild packs, and we hear them barking madly – at each other or prey, I can't be sure. I load the slingshot and Nalim keeps her gun in her hand. I hate to think what we'll face when the sun goes down. There is more to fear than WUG soldiers in this place.

As much as I want to keep walking through the night, I have to call a halt. I'm famished and we need to find food before it grows dark. She says we should keep going, but I know from my experience on long hunts that quick stops to rest and recharge make for much faster and safer travel in the long run.

I lead us through overgrown backyards looking for more remains of gardens, but all we find is more dandelions. I'm glad for any food, but it's not going to be enough. Then I hit gold: a batch of very distinct green spears shooting out of the ground. Asparagus is a perennial plant and is the only vegetable that remains in this abandoned little herb garden. My mouth waters at the thought of fire-roasted asparagus. These certainly aren't mature yet, but they'll do just fine.

"We've been going hard," I say. "We're only as good as we treat ourselves and neither of us are going to be of any use later if we don't replace the calories we're spending. Let's take a half hour break up ahead at that park and have a quick meal."

About three hundred yards ahead is an entrance to a parking lot and beyond it a new-growth forest of maples and birches. The sign says "Community Nature Preserve." I feel sorry for the people of Philadelphia if this is their idea of preserving nature, but I guess it's better than nothing. I will never understand people who live in the city.

"I'm gonna head to that little creek down there," I say. "You want to start a fire?"

"Sure, I can do that," Nalim says, bending down to gather tinder. "What's on the menu?"

I toss her the fire striker around my neck. "Not exactly sure. I'm still working on that."

I leave my bug-out bag with her and head for the creek with our canteen. I've got my slingshot and machete with me as well, in case I see squirrels, rabbits or even bigger game. My mood lifts a little. I love being in the woods, even if it's a "Community

Nature Preserve."

Creeks and streams are teaming with life this time of year. The spring rains and warming temperatures are the perfect combination for all kinds of wildlife. I'm craving crawdads, or as my Dad used to call them, "mountain shrimp." I used to love catching crawdads with Dad. The thought of it makes me miss him. He taught me how to catch them when I was only five years old and used to tell me I was the best crawdaddy catcher this side of the Mississippi. I remember how cool I thought that was. Whether I am or whether I'm not, crawdads are easy to catch, easy to cook and easy to eat, and Nalim and I can use the protein.

My feet are happy to get out of my moccasins for the first time on this trip. The cool water on my sore feet and calves and the soft sand between my toes gives new energy to my tired muscles. One at a time, I turn over rocks and watch for crawdads to shoot backward in search of another home. Before long I have a bandanna full of thirty-seven big, fat crawdads.

"Best this side of the Mississippi," I say holding up the stuffed bandanna. I imagine Dad nodding in approval somewhere.

I also refill the canteen with creek water. On the way up the bank I spot a batch of wild mint so I toss a handful of mint leaves in the canteen. Especially this close to a city, we'll have to boil the water before we can drink it so we might as well make mint tea.

By the time I get back Nalim has a great little fire going.

"How about roasted wild asparagus, mountain shrimp and mint tea?" I ask.

She smiles. "I've never heard of mountain shrimp before. How gourmet!"

"Only the best for you on this special day," I reply with a smile.

Nalim cocks her head sideways and gives me a funny look. I toss a bandanna from my bug-out bag on her lap.

"You should go down to the creek and clean up a bit," I suggest. "The water is really refreshing. I'll get the food ready."

While she's gone I weave two cattail-leaf placemats. I roast the asparagus and crawdads right on the hot coals and the smells make my mouth water. I arrange the cooked food on the placemats in a fancy pattern and sprinkle each helping with pepper grass and tart, yellow wood sorrel. The aroma from the boiling mint tea is strong even with the steady afternoon breeze. It makes me think of home. Mom loves to make wild mint tea. I feel awkward about giving Nalim the birthday gift, so I wrap it in a great burdock leaf and hide it under my bug-out bag for later. I feel nervous for her to come back. I want her to like what I've done.

Just as I finish setting everything out, Nalim pops up over the bank, with an enthusiasm that only a spit bath in a creek can give. The sun setting in the west shines directly on her and she looks stunning, even after all she's been through. She's slender and graceful, with her wet blond hair loose around her shoulders. She carries her brown leather boots in her hands and walks barefoot with her jeans rolled high above her knees. Her jacket is draped over her shoulder and she's wearing a tight brown tank top that must have been under the black t-shirt. A feeling of excitement rushes my chest and I feel happy. Even the constant ache of the bullet wound fades away, inconsequential.

"Dinner is, uh, served," I stammer. I can tell I'm blushing, which only makes me blush harder.

"I can't believe you waited," Nalim grins. "You must be

as starving as I am, and this looks delicious! Boy Scout, I am impressed." She moves her placemat closer to mine and sits down right next to me. Her leg brushes against mine and I can smell the warm sweet, scent of her.

"Well I wanted it to be special," I say awkwardly.

"You said that before. What are you talking about, Omaha?"

I like hearing her say my name.

"Because today's a special day," I reply. "It's your birthday – May 3rd. Happy Birthday!" She stops in mid-bite and looks at me with wonder. I pull her gift out from under the bug-out bag and place it in her lap.

"Are you serious? How did you know that? You're amazing!"

"I saw it on the scanner when I scanned your wrist," I explain.

Nalim's eyes well with tears. "Omaha, this is the sweetest thing anyone's ever done for me," she says. "Thank you so much."

I smile, thinking again about how much I like the way she says my name.

She carefully unfolds the burdock leaf. "Oh! This is beautiful! Where did you get this? I love it."

She pulls a clump of blonde bangs away from her eyes and pins them back with her new butterfly hair clip.

CHAPTER EIGHT

I'm not sorry I gave Nalim the hair clip, but that doesn't mean I don't feel a pang of guilt. It was meant for London, but London isn't here right now, and Nalim is, and it's her birthday. For the first time in maybe forever, I don't want to think about London just now. I want to enjoy Nalim's eyes beaming with pleasure as she tries to see her reflection on the side of the shiny metal canteen. I want to tell her it looks beautiful on her, but the words can't get out. I guess this is what some folk call "tongue-tied."

"Do you like it on me, Omaha," she laughs, striking a ridiculous girly pose with one hand on her hip and another behind her head. "Well, do you," she asks, throwing a different pose, this one blowing a kiss at me. I'm speechless.

"Omaha, are you blushing." She is clearly enjoying the effect she's having on me. I know my face is bright red. "Am I embarrassing the wild hunter?"

She strikes an even more ridiculous pose and suddenly I'm

cracking up.

"This is the best gift I've ever gotten," she says eventually when we stop laughing.

"I'm glad," is all I can say. And then Nalim gives me a big hug. She wraps her arms around mine, which makes it so that I can't really hug her back. I bend my arms at the elbow and try to turn it into a hug but it comes out incredibly weird, which makes the whole situation even more awkward.

"Now let us eat!" she declares, disentangling herself from me. I don't argue with that. We devour our dinner with many appreciative noises. While I put the fire out and repack the bug-out bag, I explain the special features of the butterfly hair clip and Nalim declares again that it's the perfect birthday present.

Within a few minutes we're headed east again, our spirits lifted with crawdad calories. We decide to follow the creek, which leads into an area too steep and rocky to be developed for housing. About half a mile down, we merge onto a natural game trail most likely created by deer that take shelter in this small patch of forest. The sun starts its descent into the horizon and casts a purple hue into the forest ahead. Luckily, the rain has held off. We will need to think about making camp soon.

I've spent more time in the woods than at home. My scout troop went hiking and camping nearly every month, and sometimes Dad or Grandpa would take me out to help me work on my Wilderness Survival badge. I wasn't good at school, but Grandpa said I was a "natural" at woods craft. To earn the merit badge I had to spend one night in the woods in a shelter I built from sticks and leaves, and start a fire on my own without matches. It was during a week away at Scout camp that I did it. When the camp director came to get me the next day, he seemed surprised when I presented him with an extra roasted squirrel. I loved Boy Scout camp, especially that year.

Scouting taught me to feel at home in the woods, and then be part of what was around me–to blend in, to smell, see, hear, taste and feel with the forest. It became a way of life for me. I belong in the woods. Like right now, the sounds and shapes of the forest tell a story about the animals that live here. The game trail we are following is well traveled and has probably been used by deer in this area for centuries. The stains leading up the old oak ahead are from the muddy belly of a raccoon that climbs in and out of a hole thirty feet up every night. The trickle of the stream below leads to a watering hole somewhere in the valley that abounds with fish and frogs. Smaller game runs that intersect with this one team with possum, skunk, rabbit and groundhog in the twilight hours of each day. The pile of walnut hulls beneath the large maple on our left tells me a squirrel lives in that tree. I'm walking, but I'm also reading the story of this forest.

But something about the story this forest is telling me doesn't seem right. I don't know what is off about it, but it's obvious that something is wrong here. We haven't seen one single animal since we came into this forest. Not one bird. Not one squirrel. Nothing. Even close to the city, this is very unusual for any woodland setting.

Grandpa and Dad could move in complete silence through the woods. Dad was amazing. Even with crunchy leaves on the ground he would only move when the wind blew to cover any slight noise he made. He taught me always to wear leather-soled moccasins because they let me feel everything on the forest floor before I bear down my full weight. I can prevent a branch from snapping because I can feel the contour of the branch on the sensitive sole of my foot. The emu soles of these moccasins

London made me are the best I've ever had – thin, but almost impossible to puncture, making them the perfect combination for traveling through the woods.

I try to travel quietly through the woods, but Nalim makes noise as she walks, oblivious to twigs snapping and branches breaking. I try to tune that out and focus all of my being on the forest around me. What is wrong? My senses are heightened and goose bumps rise up my back and arms. My ears strain to hear every sound around me.

"Something is wrong," I say quietly, holding up my hand to stop her from moving forward.

"What do you mean?" She sees my face and her eyebrows shoot up. "Omaha, you're scaring me! What's going on?"

"I can't figure out what it is, but something isn't right. Something is off. The forest is too quiet." She is silent while I listen to the troubling absence of noises around us. The fading light and forest shadows are playing tricks on my eyes, and the uneasy feeling in my gut is getting stronger. We will need to make camp soon. Our steep climb has brought us to the edge of a cliff that leads to a green valley below. The trail down is very steep, but passable, and I hope to make it down before we stop for a few hours of sleep.

Suddenly, a loud snap of a branch shatters the silence. My slingshot is automatically out and in my hand. I spin around to face the source of the noise and fully expect to see a WUG soldier. My eyes strain to make out the silhouette of something crouched in the middle of the trail about a hundred yards back. It's large, but I can't tell what it is – only that it's nothing that belongs in this forest. It knows that I know it's there, and it doesn't care. Then I hear a sound that I've only heard once before in my life, a sound I will never forget as long as I live: the low purring growl of a male mountain lion. It sends icy chills up my spine and momentarily takes the breath from my lungs. I am face to face with the most feared predator in the eastern woodlands. I know one important fact about mountain lions: the males are very territorial. This is his path and his woods. We are the trespassers. We are the prey.

Only once in my life did I ever see my grandfather show fear. We had been away from home for more than two weeks tracking a small herd of elk through the mountains. We had a shot on several cows, but Grandpa was insistent on taking the large bull. It was February and the snow was heavy that year. Tracking was easy, but they were on the move and it was hard for us to keep up with them. Finally, after walking through the night we got our shot in the morning. We were on a ridge that looked over a small meadow. The big bull was grazing. When we hit him, he took off over a small hill out of sight. We waited about an hour like we always did, to let him pass in peace, and then headed off in his direction. The blood trail was easy to follow in the fresh, white, morning snow and from the looks of it he wouldn't be far off. Just as we crested the small hill, we heard the warning purr of the mountain lion that had taken claim to our elk bull. The lion was only sixty feet away. I'll never forget the look in Grandpa's eye: fear and apology and surprise rolled into one.

"Don't run, Omaha," he said with forced calm. "Back away very slowly. We are the trespassers. This is his woods."

After a couple hours we went back and took what was left of the meat. It was the first time in my life that I was not at the top of the food chain. I did not like that feeling at all.

This time is different. This time there is no backing away slowly, because we have a ravine at our backs. There is no dead elk bull to appease him. There is also no time to dip and load munti. Nalim's .22 revolver won't stop him. He'll be on us in seconds. The pack will slow me down and I will need all of the speed I can summon. I tear off my bug-out bag and hand it to her and take off at a sprint.

As soon as I move, the large cat lunges forward. He knows now that I am reacting to his battle call.

"Run! " I yell with breath I can't spare. "The valley!" I scream.

Nalim is frozen in terror.

"RUN!" I can't afford to keep looking back. It's slowing me down, but I need to know she's moving. "NOW!"

I can't see what she does because now I have to focus on the ground in front of me. If I trip and fall, I'm dead. I hear the big cat thundering through the woods behind me. His instinct is to chase and kill. I'm charging ahead with all the strength I have. I look back for a brief second and I panic at how close he is to me—just a few yards away. I register the detail of a yellow collar around his neck and realize he is one of the zoo animals. That makes it worse – he probably has reason to hate the smell of humans. He's staked his claim to this small patch of woods. I'm trying to manage my fear but I'm having trouble thinking straight. I'm sprinting faster than I've ever run before and hoping for some advantage.

Ahead I can see a deep ravine about thirty feet across. It appears to be an old construction gravel pit. It's too far to jump. My heart sinks. I only have a few seconds until I either leap to my death into the gravel pit or his front claws rip into my back. He will go for my neck because they always go for the neck. Halfway across the ravine there is a large grapevine hanging from a tree on the other side. I follow the vine with my eyes and see that it's rooted on my side of the ravine. I will not be able to swing across with it rooted to the ground on my side. As I'm filing away this data, I am at the edge and the cat's hot breath is right on me. I leap.

Claws shred my right calf and blood fills my moccasin, but I travel through the air and grab for the grapevine with my uninjured arm while my right arm yanks the machete from its sheath. As my left hand grabs the upper part of the vine, my right slices through the vine below my handhold. The vine surges forward with the momentum of my flying body and I almost lose my grip. The vine shifts and loosens from the treetop under my full weight. With all my might I throw my machete to the other side of the ravine so that my right hand is free to grab the cliff that's barreling toward me.

I am not going to clear the ravine so I brace for impact into the rock wall on the opposite side. For a second everything goes black. I can't breathe. I know this feeling. I was kicked in the chest by a horse once and it knocked the wind out of me. I hold to the vine for dear life while my lungs struggle to work. When I can take a gasping breath, I pull myself up, one hand over the other. It's ten agonizing feet to the edge of the ravine. Adrenaline fuels me, but it's starting to fade a little and the pain of my calf is so bad I don't even care that my gunshot wound has torn open and is bleeding again. I haul myself onto the top of the far side of the ravine and barely fight back the panic at the sight of my shredded, bloody calf.

The cat paces on the other side and screams with frustration and claws the air in my direction. He paces back and forth as if formulating a strategic plan then turns and races along the ravine's edge and out of sight. For the first time, I look down into the ravine and what I see makes me shudder. It is lined with jagged rocks and rusty old construction machinery. I would never have survived a fall.

I'm not out of danger yet – not by a long shot. This is his woods. He isn't going to be stopped by a ravine. I am certain he knows a way across. I grab my machete and slice a chunk of fabric from my undershirt to tie around my calf and staunch the flow of blood. His claws ripped through my heavy pants and skin like they were nothing. He is coming for me.

What do I do? Think! I feel panic rising in my chest. Think!

A loud screech from the branches above startles me. I turn my head and look up to see a large eagle perched in a monster cedar tree a few feet back. Just as our eyes meet, he spreads his wings and flies away into the forest.

"Cedar – yes! That's perfect!"

I slam the thick blade of my machete into the huge cedar tree and quickly peel huge strips of cedar bark away from the tree. Native people used cedar bark to make fishing line that could pull one-hundred-pound fish from the depths of the ocean. If they can use it to pull fish out of the ocean, maybe I can use it to pull a mountain lion into a ravine. My hands are shaking while I work. I can hear the big cat tearing through the scrub brush. He has surely made it to this side, and he's on his way to finish off his kill. My blood is on his claws and he's hungry. I wrap several pieces of the bark together to make it stronger and manage to fashion a big noose, which I hang loosely from the low-hanging branches in the direction where I calculate the big cat will be coming. The big loop hangs wide open across an opening in the bushes right in front of me. I tie the other end around the biggest boulder I can find. Dragging my bleeding leg and sobbing with pain, I manage to push it right up to the edge of the ravine.

I lie down a couple yards back from the noose and place both feet on the boulder. I can see the cat's silhouette in the late dusk light. He's running along the edge of the ravine toward me. He must run through the noose. The yellow collar stands out. I take a deep breath and thank the cedar. I thank the grapevine. I thank the eagle. If I have to die now, at least Nalim will be safe.

He's just fifteen feet away, racing confidently toward me. As soon as his head passes through the noose I let loose a scream to give me strength and I shove the boulder over the edge with all of my might. Just before the lion reaches me, the falling boulder yanks him sideways and pulls his shoulder to the ground. Please God, don't let the cedar line break! I fend off a clawing strike with my machete. The scream of claw against metal is like nothing I've ever heard before. It resonates through the chasm below. The cat scrambles at the edge of the cliff with all four paws, trying to fight against the overwhelming weight of the boulder pulling at his neck, but it's too much. I wish it didn't have to be like this. He disappears over the edge and I hear the crash a few seconds later. For several minutes I can hear noises from the dying predator until finally the forest is completely silent.

CHAPTER NINE

It is pitch-dark when I regain consciousness. Something cold and wet hits me on the face. I must have passed out right after the lion fell. I know I'm lying by the ravine and I should be careful, but I feel confused and disoriented. I have no idea how much blood I've lost. The familiar sound of rain pattering on the leafy canopy above me drowns out any hope of calling to Nalim for help. First one, then two, now hundreds of cold, sloppy raindrops show no mercy on my battered and bruised body. I open my mouth to drink some – at least there's that. Thunder rumbles overhead and a streak of lightning lights up the forest long enough for me to notice a small rock outcropping a few yards into the woods. Maybe it will offer some protection from the pouring rain. I figure it's better than nothing. I drag myself over and am shocked at how weak I am and how much pain I'm in. I'm gasping for breath when I get to the rocks and pull myself tight in against the side of the biggest one. The rain drips from the ledge above me and I welcome the cool water into my parched mouth.

I'm nearly too exhausted to move, but I force myself to cut another strip of fabric from my undershirt and blindly replace the blood-soaked bandage. My calf throbs in pain, and I can only hope the cuts are clean.

It's a long, cold night of pain. I'm wet and shivering and worried – about London and Rake, of course; about Nalim; about Mom and Macy. And tonight I'm worried about me. I'm in pretty bad shape and I still have miles to go. And when I get to Philadelphia, what then? It's too overwhelming to think about.

So much has happened to me in such a short amount of time. I haven't even started to come to terms with how I feel about killing five men (although, technically, Fink killed himself). I make myself think about it because it distracts me from the pain in my calf and arm. Do I feel guilty about their deaths?

I don't – especially not the two men who were attacking the woman and her daughter. They totally deserved to die. I deliberately make myself remember the details of the killings. I go over in my mind and see that I had no choice. They were armed and fully intending to kill anyone in their way, so I had a right to defend those helpless women and myself. I feel a little better about it after a while.

But what about the first two soldiers? They shot me in the arm and would have killed me or turned me into a slave. And they hurt Nalim, so I guess I don't feel bad about their deaths, either.

I don't feel the least bit bad about Fink's death. I just wish I didn't have those vivid memories of it in my head!

I guess the only death I do feel bad about is the lion's. His aggression wasn't personal. He was an animal acting on instinct. He was predator; I was prey. He was going to kill me so he could eat me, and don't I do that all the time when I hunt? The thought of his magnificent, broken body at the bottom of the ravine makes me sad.

"Think about something happy," I order myself.

My mind immediately goes to Grandpa and Dad, and all the great times we had together tracking, hunting, fishing, being in the wilderness together and all of our times in scouting. I remember Grandpa's stories about the ancestors helping him when he was bitten by a rattlesnake and I suddenly wonder if the eagle I saw earlier was one of my ancestors coming back to help me. I wish Dad and Grandpa were with me now. I wish I could talk to them. I clutch the machete tight against my chest.

"Maybe Grandpa was right about you, ol' boy – the steadiness of that oak and the force of that lightning. You've saved me more than once on this trip. Now, we just have to get to London."

I'm not quite sure if I pass out or fall asleep, but tonight I dream of Nalim lying under a tarp in the valley below. I dream that Gi-Nong warriors are hunting her as payback for Dad killing so many of their people. I try to catch up to them, but they are too far ahead of me. After days of tracking I finally find their camp, but it's too late. Nalim is tied to a pole and a hunting party of Gi-Nong warriors surrounds her in a big circle, slingshots loaded and drawn with lizard-poisoned munti. I scream as loud as I can for them to stop. In a moment that seems like eternity my eyes meet hers.

She mouths, "You can't save everyone, Omaha."

The Gi-Nong warriors send their dogs to stop me and their frothing jaws tear at my legs and feet. The very real pain from dogs tearing at my flesh yanks me from my sleep.

"Get off me!" I yell, finding a very real possum clawing and licking at the bloody bandage around my calf. One swift kick sends it reeling across the forest floor with a chilling hiss. I shudder, because it looks like a vampire possum with its teeth and chin dripping with my blood.

"Get outta here before I kill and eat you," I warn. It scurries off over the hill.

It's dawn and the rain has stopped. The rock ledge above me is still dripping so I take a few minutes to rehydrate. Our scoutmaster drilled this into us: proper hydration is very important, especially with my recent blood loss. The ravine from last night looks much more intimidating in daylight. I peek over and see the big cat on the rocks below and feel thankful it's not me down there.

I cut myself a sturdy walking stick and slowly make my way along the edge of the ravine to find where the big cat crossed over. About fifty yards down I find a huge sycamore tree that has fallen across. He knew this was here. This is his woods. This was his woods. I cross and make my way back to where I left Nalim. I scan the valley below and wonder where in the world she is.

After a few minutes of studying the landscape, I see a glimmer from the far side of the valley. I dismiss it as the sun reflecting off a puddle of rain from last night, but then I see the flash again, then again. It's too bright and the sequence is too regular to be natural. Then it hits me: Nalim's butterfly hair clip! She's using it to signal me. She has my binoculars and maybe she's been watching this spot and waiting for me. I sight a landmark near the flashing light and start down the trail toward the valley.

The searing pain in my calf is slowing me down and I hobble downhill, each jolting step is excruciating. Whenever I start to give in to it and decide to sit down to rest I imagine London trapped in Philadelphia. I do stop to check my leg and the bleeding has stopped, but it's swollen up to twice its normal size. I need to clean it soon, before infection sets in. My arm is also killing me. It throbs with each step as well. As I'm walking, I notice broken hanging branches every twenty feet or so. Did Nalim leave these as trail markers for me to follow? She has more skills than she let on. It's confirmed a few minutes later when I see sticks and rocks arranged in an arrow to point in the direction she headed. A few minutes later there's an even larger arrow made from pine cones. Despite my physical agony, I'm smiling. That girl is smart!

It takes me a full hour to go about a mile, and then I smell the very welcome aroma of a campfire. I cross through a dense forest of young pines, which reminds me of the one at home. When I come out the other side I can see smoke climbing from the top of a little shelter near a stream.

"Omaha! Thank God!" screams Nalim. She is running toward me. "You made it! I was so worried!"

I wave, but am too exhausted to scream back. It's everything I can do to keep from collapsing. Then she slams into me and wraps her arms around me. "I'm so glad you made it!" But I'm gasping in pain. She quickly lets go of me. "Oh my God, you're hurt!"

"You should see the other guy," I say with a weak smile.

"Come on," she says. "Now it's time for me to take care of you like you've been taking care of me."

"Nice lean-to shelter," I comment. I'm actually really impressed with the shelter. She built the frame from driftwood

from the creek and covered the top with thick layers of
reed grass that grows by the millions down in this valley. As
comfortable as it looks, we really need to keep moving.

"It's water tight, too," she replies proudly. "Not a drip last
night."

"I wish I could say the same," I reply, ringing water from
the bottom of my wool hunting shirt.

She ushers me under the lean-to roof onto a thick pile of
reed grass. It's surprisingly comfortable and hard to resist. I look
over to the fire and notice two big rainbow trout cooking on the
hot coals.

"You've been busy," I say, eyeing the trout.

"It's easy when you have good tools," she replies pointing to
her butterfly hair clip. "I used the fishing line and hook from
this."

"Macy would be proud," I say with a smile.

She would be proud. Nalim has used her gift extensively
already and it has worked very well. I miss my little sister. I miss
my mom. I almost died last night, but now I'm safe. I lay my
head back on the soft reed grass mattress and close my eyes.

"Omaha...Omaha...," I hear Nalim say.

"Sorry," I reply. "I must have dozed off."

"I'd say," she replies. "You've been asleep for two hours."

"Two hours!" I exclaim, rolling head first out of the shelter
and onto the sand. "We have to get going. Why didn't you wake
me?"

"Calm down. You were exhausted. We wouldn't have gotten
very far before you'd have passed out on me. You needed the
rest and you know it. And while you were sleeping I patched
you up."

I look down and see that she cleaned and dressed the

cuts on my calf. I can't believe I slept through it – I really was exhausted. I have to admit I feel a lot better now. The clean white gauze sticks out like a sore thumb against the rest of my dirty body. She also bandaged my arm. I don't ask her about infection because it won't make any difference. I'd already used up the last of the antibiotic cream. I'll use the penicillin I stole from the WUG truck as a last resort.

"I saved you the big one." She hands me the cooked trout on a driftwood plank.

I thank her and devour it while Nalim packs up the bug-out bag and scatters the coals from the fire.

She insists on carrying the pack, and I don't argue because it's going to take all my strength to walk the rest of the way to Philadelphia.

We'll be there today! I almost can't believe it. Nalim talks excitedly about where her father hid boats on the Schuylkill River. That's where we'll part ways.

The thought makes me unhappy. It's ironic that just yesterday I was considering how I could leave her behind, but today I can't imagine not having her beside me. Although I've only known her for two days, I feel closer to her than anyone but my family, and London, of course.

When we consult the map, I'm relieved to see we're much closer to Philadelphia than I thought. A major highway runs close by, which means we can move faster. But it also means we'll have to be extra careful not to run into WUG patrols. I decide the best strategy is to travel east along the valley stream, which will eventually spill into the Delaware River. Then we'll follow the Delaware River north to the Schuylkill River, which runs right up through the middle of Philadelphia. Nalim will show me where the storm drain tunnels dump into the river

from Philadelphia and then she will head back south down
the Schuylkill River toward New Jersey to find her dad. I will
head north alone through the drainage tunnels into downtown
Philadelphia to find London and Rake. I know that sounds a lot
easier than it's going to be.

Travel along the river is excruciatingly painful with my calf
in its current state. The soft mud and rocky terrain is torturous.
Nalim helps as much as possible, but she is already weighed
down by the bug-out bag. I'm thankful she's offered to carry it
because I don't know if my calf could handle the extra weight.

It's near noon when we reach the banks of the Delaware
River. It's the largest river I've ever seen. Right away I notice
WUG patrol boats puttering around upstream and decide
we should use some of my natural camouflage techniques to
reduce our chances of being spotted. We smear river mud all
over our bodies and stick on handfuls of forest debris such as
leaves, twigs and grasses. Nalim is nearly invisible from only
ten feet away and blends in almost perfectly with the shoreline,
except for her piercing blue eyes, of course. She's beautiful even
covered in river mud. I feel a little unfaithful to London for
thinking it.

The sudden reverb of a loud speaker makes us freeze. It
reminds me of the one they used at summer camp to make
announcements. It's coming from one of the WUG boats a few
hundred yards away. My heart sinks. I'm sure they spotted us.
But thankfully, the motor fires up and surges the boat upstream
and away from us.

"HALT!" a voice barks through the boat's speaker system.
"HALT!"

We move as fast as we can around the bend ahead to see
what's gotten their attention. A small rowboat packed with

people ranging from young children to old women is floating down the middle of the Delaware River. An old man in the bow is waving a white t-shirt attached to an oar – a universal sign of surrender, no matter what language you speak. A metal-on-metal screech jerks my attention back to the WUG boat as I see a soldier spin a turreted machine gun toward the rowboat. Without hesitation, the soldier pulls back the breach bolt to engage the weapon and opens fire on the surrendering group of Philadelphia refugees.

"Noooooooooo!" It's me – I'm screaming hysterically. Nalim pulls me to the ground behind a rotting log.

"Omaha, quiet!" she says urgently. "You'll get us both killed! There's nothing we can do."

After everything we've seen on this trip, this slaughter of innocent people is more than I can bear. Tears course down my cheeks. "They were just trying to get somewhere safe," I'm saying. "They're just trying to survive! Old people and women and children!"

She rubs my back and says nothing, but I know she has seen things like this before. Now I understand: this is what turned her into a rebel.

We move forward with more determination. London is in the city, and the stark truth about what she's facing makes me sick to my stomach. I hate the WUG and will show no mercy to any of them. I will kill as many WUG soldiers as possible because this is war they started.

We're only a mile or so from the city and I can hear more gunfire and explosions in the distance. A rancid, chemical, burning smell fills the air and irritates my nostrils. We're hugging the bank of the river, but now there are more buildings towering above us than trees. Helicopters buzz overhead, flying to and from the city. WUG vehicles appear every few minutes on the road on the embankment above us. Soon, there will be no trees and we will be forced into the open.

"Careful!" Nalim hisses. I look down and jump back. A dead body has floated to shore in front of us. We step over it with a shudder and nearly stumble over another three feet away. Dead bodies litter the banks here. Each one has at least one bullet hole that I can see, but I stop looking after the fifth. There's no need to solve a mystery. These people were all shot by the WUG.

So many people are dead. So many people are suffering. All of this is much more horrifying than I ever imagined. A ferocious explosion in the distance rattles the ground and a pillar of smoke and fire rises above the city's horizon. Nalim grabs my good arm and I can feel her trembling.

"Is it the bombs?" she asks in a whisper.

I listen for a minute but there are no more explosions. "I don't think so," I whisper back. "In New York and Chicago the sky was full of drones when the bombing started."

That's the first good news I've had all day. I may actually have gotten here in time to get London and Rake out before it's too late!

I've never been pushed to my physical limits like this before. Even when Grandpa and I used to haul two hundred pounds of elk meat on our backs through the mountains it wasn't this hard. Nalim and I are completely spent. We haven't had enough calories for all the energy we've burned. The harsh, mucky terrain combined with my near-crippling injuries has made this last stretch of travel the most demanding yet. I don't want to stop – I want to charge in and find London – but I will have to rest before the tunnels. My journey is far from over and I need to be prepared for the what's to come.

"This looks like our last patch of decent woods," I tell Nalim. "I need to stop and refresh our supplies."

Inside the city limits, I don't expect to find any food, and from the looks of things, the water will be too polluted to drink.

I throw my machete into at an old, gnarly maple tree. The point slices deep into the wood. After a few seconds, a small bead of liquid oozes out from around the blade and draws a thin wet line on its way down the dusty gray bark. Grandpa and I used to collect gallons and gallons of maple tree sap in early spring and boil it down to make maple syrup. We would also tap the sap to drink on long winter hunts in the mountains. Maple tree sap contains sugars and nutrients and is one of my favorite wilderness drinks.

Before long the deep gouge is dripping like a leaky faucet. I stick in a small leaf to wick the sap away from the tree and position my canteen underneath to catch the flow of sweet, drinkable liquid. Within a few minutes my canteen is full to the brim. The woods are full of trash and garbage carried in from high floods. I scavenge a couple of decent plastic bottles and fill those with maple sap as well. I doubt there will be any potable water inside the city limits so it's important I carry enough for me, London and Rake. Nalim fills three bottles for her own journey south.

I spot a small flock of pigeons resting in a bush at the edge of the forest and silently kill four of them with clean shots to the head using my slingshot and non-poisoned munti. I find that city pigeons are not as leery of humans as wild birds, so they are surprisingly easy to hunt. The silence of my slingshot makes it possible this close to WUG patrols. Nalim finds a plastic bag and gathers the young, edible, basswood leaves I show her while I field dress the four birds.

Using a typical fire to cook the birds is too risky. The smoke might draw unwanted attention to our little patch of woods. Instead, I use an old Native American trick Grandpa taught me called a dakota fire hole. I dig two holes in the ground about two feet apart from each other, both eighteen inches deep. The soil is loose and damp from last night's rain, and I can dig both holes using only my left arm and a sharp digging stick. The first hole is twelve inches across and the other six inches across. I then connect the two holes with an underground tunnel the size of my forearm. I start a fire in the larger hole and it pulls the oxygen it needs through the smaller hole. This makes for a very discreet fire that is both hidden underground and nearly smokeless. I lay some green basswood sticks across the larger hole as a cooking surface and place the pigeons on them like a mini barbeque grill. I notice I'm running a little low on munti so while the pigeons cook I carve fifteen more out of swamp oak and tuck them in my pack.

While I carve munti, Nalim fashions herself a makeshift backpack out of fabric from an old couch, some scrap netting and three sticks. I watch as she packs in the three plastic bottles of maple sap, some stuffing from the couch pillow for fire tinder, an old sheet of plastic, some extra rope and a metal hubcap that I presume will serve as a cooking and boiling pot. I'm impressed. She's very resourceful.

As the birds cook, I take stock of my supplies. Entering Philadelphia exhausted and low on resources is a death sentence. My injuries will already handicap me more than I am comfortable with. As an afterthought, I fashion another ten munti out of scrap metal pieces salvaged from an old couch frame. Unlike my wooden ones, these will pierce the heavy WUG overcoats. It's hard to use my right arm, but Nalim comes over to help without my needing to ask.

I can't help but watch her. She's watching me watch her, but I don't care. She doesn't seem to care either. Soon I won't be able to watch her anymore and I'm soaking it up while I can. She pulls her hair back and readjusts the butterfly clip and her tank top pulls tight against her chest. I don't know if it's the exhaustion or the fact that I know I won't see her again, but I keep watching anyway. The .22 revolver rests against her hip bone, which now shows in the gap between her pants and tank top. My chest tightens and my breathing quickens. She's allowing me to watch. Her eyes tell me it's okay with her that I want to watch.

The birds cook fast and we each eat one, devouring it quickly as we have all our meals. It's not enough, but it's something. I feel stronger after just a few bites. I wrap up the two extra birds.

"Here," I say. "Let me see if you've got all the gear you need." I do want to help her, but I also want an excuse to be closer to her. We sit together and go through my bug-out bag and I give her the fixed-blade knife I took from the WUG soldier who held her captive; one of the cooked pigeons; the fire striker from around my neck; six water purification tablets; a pair of wool socks; and the Hershey's bar.

"Chocolate! Where did you get this?" Nalim exclaims softly. "You've been holding out on me."

"I've been saving it for the right moment, but our moments together will be over soon, I guess." That was nearly poetic for me. Maybe spending all this time with a girl has been good for me after all.

She steps in close to me, picks the least muddy spot on my cheek and gives me a soft kiss. "I'll never forget what you've done for me, Boy Scout," she whispers in my ear, leaning on my chest. I know she can feel my heart pounding, but again, I don't care.

"I'll never forget you either," I whisper back. I gently fold my arms around her and she looks up at me, her sapphire eyes shining. Time seems to stand still. I haven't felt this way since London and I kissed in the meadow. I want to kiss Nalim, but now I'm thinking about London and how she's trapped in that godforsaken city waiting for me to rescue her and here I am in the arms of another girl. Even though London has never been my girlfriend, I feel in my soul that I'm betraying her by wanting to kiss Nalim.

Nalim must wonder why I'm just standing there, not kissing her. I'm 17 years old and I've only ever kissed one girl. I want to, of course – I want to a lot! But I'm confused with longing and guilt.

"What's wrong," she asks.

"Everything's wrong," I reply. "Starting with you leaving me."

I realize in that moment that I'm scared of losing them both. I can't protect London in Philadelphia. I can't protect Nalim wherever she's going next. Not being able to take care of the people I love is the one thing I fear the most. I feel as if I'm losing control and failing everyone.

"Omaha, I—"

"Just forget it," I say, releasing her with some regret. "Nalim, it's time. We need to get going."

I carry my pack because now Nalim has a pack of her own to carry. The extra burden distracts me from thinking too much about the moment we almost had back there. I'm thankful she isn't making me talk about it. Talking about my emotions isn't easy, especially when I don't even understand them myself.

Soon, we have other things on our minds. The Schuylkill dumps into the Delaware about a hundred yards away, around a slight bend. We hug tight to the scrub brush. There is constant WUG traffic only a few feet away from us and we have to crouch down every time a truck passes. If one soldier happens to look out the window, we'll be seen. The pile-up of dead bodies is thicker than ever here. I have to put the fact that these are human beings in a compartment somewhere at the back of my head and heart. I don't have the luxury to think about it right now.

There are no signs of civilians trying to leave the city anywhere. This makes me very uneasy. On the opposite side of the embankment, I do see living people for the first time and it's not good news. There is a WUG construction crew operating big bulldozers to dig huge pits. A line of dump trucks pull up one by one and dumps their contents into piles that are then pushed into the pits and buried. Large cranes also use big metal talons to pick up piles of trash and drop it from high in the air into some of the pits.

I sift through my bug-out bag to find my binoculars so I can get a closer look. It takes a second for my mind to register what my eyes are seeing. The trucks aren't dumping trash; they are dumping bodies. They are pushing and burying big piles of human bodies like garbage. I look away to prevent myself from throwing up.

"What is it?" asks Nalim.

"People," I reply. "People they've killed."

I can't take my eyes off the long line of dump trucks pulling up, dumping bodies and driving off again. I have no words. I will never forget this as long as I live.

A warm hand slips into mine. I shoot Nalim a grateful look. Without speaking we continue upstream along tree line, hand in hand.

"There it is," Nalim whispers, pointing ahead. "Dad hid the boats up that little creek just south of where you see the storm drains coming out."

I see about a dozen or so storm drainage culverts jutting out of the concrete above the river. Rainwater from the city streets makes its way to the river through these drainage tunnels. I will make my way into the heart of Philadelphia by crawling up through them.

In only a few minutes we reach the creek. It's more of a marsh than a creek. I can see why her father chose this spot. No one would ever crawl through this mess voluntarily. Large evergreen cedars grow along the edges, which provide excellent cover year round. I help Nalim push aside sweeping cedar bows at the edge of the marsh. To my surprise, under the drooping branches sit five camouflaged aluminum john boats. Olive-drab netting covers them.

"These aren't supposed to be here," Nalim says with a perplexed look on her face. "These are the escape boats. They were going to use these boats to leave when things got bad. They aren't supposed to be here," she says again, bewildered. And then the truth sinks in. "He never made it out. My dad is still in Philadelphia."

CHAPTER TEN

I'm ashamed for feeling a little leap of happiness that now maybe Nalim will travel with me into the city. It is completely selfish of me. Her father may not be alive, and if he is, he's in terrible danger. But the truth is I wasn't ready to say goodbye to her and I'll be very glad to have her knowledge of Philadelphia. I'm out of my element here in the city and am realizing that I've grossly underestimated the nearly impossible task ahead of finding London and Rake in this war-torn place.

"Nalim, if he's still alive we will find him," I reply. "I promise."

This seems to make Nalim feel better, but as soon as I say it I wish I could take it back. How can I possibly promise that? I can't add finding Nalim's father to my agenda. I need to worry about London and Rake. They need to remain my priority. Dad always told me not to make promises I can't keep.

"Let's get on with it, then," Nalim says, her face pinched and drawn with the effort of not crying.

The two hundred yards between the cedar swamp and the tunnels is nothing but wide-open concrete. Trying to cross that gap in daylight will be a suicide mission. WUG soldiers patrol the road above the tunnels, and several well camouflaged watch towers have been constructed in nearby trees for 360-degree surveillance of the area. We're so close, yet so far away. It's like showing someone dying of thirst in the desert a cup of water, but not letting them drink. The frustration is beyond description. Judging by the sizable pile of bodies at the base of the concrete slope below the tunnels, the WUG's system seems to be very effective at preventing refugees from escaping through the tunnels. Getting into the tunnels is going to prove equally difficult, if we even get a chance.

***

"Omaha, look!"

We've been hiding near the boats for 45 minutes, trying to figure out how to get into Philadelphia when Nalim points to one of the tunnels. I train my binoculars on it. A middle-aged man wearing a red baseball cap peeks out and then cautiously steps outside and looks around. I glass the towers with my binoculars and notice that all three WUG watchmen have their weapons aimed right at him. For some reason, they are holding fire. The man retreats back into the tunnel and returns a few moments later with three more refugees. Gaunt and dirty, they carefully begin to descend the concrete slope toward the cedar swamp where we are hidden. One of the men walks with a crutch. If they make it here, the guards will come for them and our cover will be blown. Again, I glass the towers. My heart is pounding so hard I can barely keep the binoculars still against my eyes. I watch as one of the guards pulls back the lever on his rifle and loads a round from the magazine. I pan back to the refugees. They are about halfway here. They've gone too far to go back. I want to scream to them to run, but it's no use. Nalim pulls the binoculars away from my face just as we hear the shots ring out. I'm grateful I didn't have a closer view because it's bad enough without it.

The red baseball cap flies through the air and lands a few yards away from the refugees. A second shot from a different angle splits the crutch in half and that man falls to his knees. The refugees huddle together. The guards are just playing with them like this is some kind of video game. This is a game to them. If you're going to kill them, just kill them, I think to myself. What we're watching is sadistic.

Nalim is moaning and I put my left arm around her and hold her face in my shoulder while she sobs uncontrollably. I close my eyes. After several more shots and the sound of laughter and cheers from the hidden towers, the carnage is over.

"Don't look," I whisper to Nalim, but I don't take my own advice. The refugees are sprawled on the concrete slope, dead.

***

Several hours of waiting are in front of us. We can't make our move until night. Nalim settles on my shoulder and falls into a restless sleep. Feeling her warm, soft body next to mine is so nice. I've never had this kind of physical interaction with London. There was always an unspoken barrier between us when it came to touching. I always thought it was because we were waiting for someday, but the usual doubts drift through my head. Maybe it's because London doesn't like me that way. Rationally, I know that could be true, but my gut says she does. She was scared of it, and that's why she had to go away. If this journey doesn't prove that I will never abandon her, I don't know what will.

When I last saw her, we were both 15. We were around the same height then, but I've grown a good six inches and I've filled out. I wonder what it will be like to see her. I wonder what she'll think of me.

I don't know many girls. I haven't had a lot of experience with people in general. Nalim seems to like me, so that's a good sign. I guess I'm not completely unfortunate looking if a girl as beautiful as she is could want to kiss me.

I must have drifted off because Nalim is shaking me awake. It's dusk now, and soon it will be dark. We each drink a full bottle of maple sap. I'm tempted to eat the cooked pigeon, but I know I might need it later. I'd trade a year of my life for some aspirin. Willow bark has a pain-relieving chemical similar to aspirin when chewed but there's not a willow in sight. My leg and arm are competing for my attention with alternating stabs of pain every time my heart beats. I hope this is just what healing feels like, but I doubt it. Infection is more likely, but I can't let myself worry about that now.

"Let's go!" Nalim whispers, frustrated with the waiting.

The silence and growing darkness has a way of fostering a belief that the coast is clear, but we both know it isn't. We have to wait until it's true night. While we wait, we talk in whispers about where we'll go. She is sure we'll find ally rebels in the tunnels that will recognize her and help us. She describes how the rebels use the tunnels to organize and hide from the WUG. She says they hold rallies in some of the larger underground utility rooms.

The sound of explosions and gunfire seem to pick up once night sets in. I try not to think about it. I have to stay positive.

Hiding in the cedar marsh, we are food for mosquitoes. The mud we slathered on earlier makes my skin feel cracked

and dry and it's not keeping the skeeters off, so I apply a fresh
coat of stinking mud. Nalim hesitates, but then does the same.
Unfortunately, it makes no difference to the mosquitoes, which
attack us with glee. "That's it; I'm going right now even if I get
shot," Nalim stands.

I believe her, and maybe she's right. It's now or never. The
sky is illuminated every few minutes with the flash of distant
explosions. The moon is too bright, illuminating the concrete
slope surprisingly well. Small clouds move across the night
sky and provide short-lived moments of dark cover. We take
one of these opportunities to scurry up the concrete slope. As
we approach the dead refugees, the moon begins to sneak out
from behind the small cloud. Within seconds we will be fully
exposed.

"Lie down on them!" I whisper, dropping down on top
of one of the dead refugees, matching my arms and legs to
his. Nalim settles into position on one of the women just as
the moonlight exposes our part of the slope. I feel completely
exposed and vulnerable, but no gunshots ring out. We are still
and silent, and it feels like an eternity before another cloud
creeps in front of the moon to block its bright glow. Nalim and
I spider-crawl our way into the tunnel, clasping each other's
hands when we finally make it safely into the dark opening. My
heart is beating so fast I have to take a few calming deep breaths
to bring it back to normal. She has warned me that sound
travels in the tunnels so we don't speak, but I silently signal her
to wait.

I pull out one of the metal munti I made from couch wire
in the woods earlier. I can see a bright orange cigarette ember
in the closest guard tower, about fifty yards away. I've never
attempted a shot this far and certainly not at night, but I think

I can do it. I dip the munti in the grape jelly jar. It takes me a few seconds to calculate the correct angle, and then I launch the munti in a high arch toward the bright ember. A few seconds pass and then suddenly the glowing tip falls like a shooting star to the ground and I can hear an agonizing scuffle from the direction of the tower.

That was for the refugees, I say to myself. If their spirits are still hanging around, I hope they know some of their deaths have been avenged. Nalim nods in approval. I realize that I've now killed out of vengeance and not self-defense. I don't feel any guilt.

I pass my headlamp over to Nalim and she takes the lead. I trust Nalim, but I don't like the fact that I now must rely on her. It's been a long time since I needed anyone but myself for my own survival. She grips the revolver and heads toward downtown Philadelphia.

Walking on the concrete tunnel floor jars my wounded calf with each step. It's taking a toll on my endurance. Nalim is just short enough not to need to bend over to walk, but I have to crouch, and my back starts to hurt after a few minutes. Several times she has to wait up for me, and I feel self-conscious about slowing us down.

Very quickly, I start to hate these tunnels. The air in here is foul, with a chemical smell and it burns my eyes and throat. Several inches of water cover the tunnel floor and moisture seeps through my leather moccasins. At each intersection Nalim checks a series of markings scratched on the wall. In some places they're painted. I recognize them as blazes, like the ones Grandpa and I used to mark old hunting trails. If I wasn't so uncomfortable and tired I could probably figure out what they're saying, but I don't have it in me right now. I follow

Nalim like a hopelessly lost puppy. After forty-five minutes we get to a metal door, and on the other side is an old utility room. I want to shout Hallelujah because now I can stand up. My back has been screaming at me for a mile.

The room appears to be a makeshift conference room. In the corner sits a large table and six folding chairs. Papers, food wrappers, empty water bottles and spent ammunition casings litter the floor. A large shipping crate full of gas masks is half-open below a well-marked map of the tunnel system, which is duct-taped to the wall. Several pictures of WUG commanders are also taped to the wall. Some are crossed out with large red Xs. One picture in particular is hung above the rest, as if more important. It's of a man in his 50s. His hair and mustache are dark -- too dark to be natural I think. His face is hard and angry, and his blue eyes look cruel. His jaws and brows protrude. He's wearing a uniform I don't recognize, khaki with red braided epaulets. His expression is part sneer, part scowl. Someone threw a dart at the photo, right at his head.

"Who's this," I ask Nalim.

"That's Public Enemy #1," she says. "This scum and his mercenaries are in charge of WUG command in Philly. They call him "The General." Tacca is his name. He was a US General and sold secrets to enemies of the U.S. He was court-martialed and put in military prison, but when the WUG showed up they let him out and gave him a promotion."

"He's an American!" I'm horrified at the thought of one of our own doing this. Was the WUG soldier I just killed also American?

I hear a splash of someone walking through the tunnels. I quickly draw a munti and aim it toward the door. Nalim turns off the light and we're plunged into darkness. I remember where the large metal filing cabinet stands and I creep over and get myself behind it.

The door opens and a light shines in from a headlamp. I can just make out the shape of a gigantic figure blocking the doorway and I hear the undeniable sound of a shell being racked in a pump shotgun.

Just before I send my munti home, Nalim screams, "Lemrac, don't shoot! Lemrac! It's me, Nalim! Omaha, don't shoot!"

I hesitate, and so does the person with the gun, so that's a good sign. I hear a match being struck. An oil lamp mounted to the wall casts a bright glow on the goliath man blocking the doorway. I've never seen anyone quite like him. He looks like a character from a comic book. His black tactical pants are tucked into tightly laced shin-high combat boots. He's not wearing a shirt, but several shotgun bandoleers loaded with shells wrap around and cover most of his upper body. His bulging muscles gleam in the flickering light. Black diagonal lines of paint or soot decorate his face and shaved head. Makeshift metal spikes wrap across each set of knuckles and a large knife is strapped to his right thigh. He repositions the gas mask that dangles around his neck and salutes Nalim like I've seen soldiers in movies salute their superior officers.

"Nalim, ma'am?" I'm surprised by his thick Russian accent. "We thought you were dead. Where did you come from? And who is this with you?"

"This is the Boy Scout who saved me," she says. "His name is Omaha. You can trust him. He's come to rescue his friends."

He studies me for a moment and I study him back. The only word that comes to mind when I see Lemrac is "warrior." Solid muscle, armed to the teeth, scars on his arms and one on his face, long healed. But mostly he's just supremely confident. I hope I never have to fight him. He would tear me apart. He sees that I see that this is true, and then he slides his gun back into its holster and I take my hand of my machete handle and give him a nod. Lemrac turns his attention back to Nalim.

"Falco must hear that you're back."

"Dad's still alive!" Nalim sags with relief. She grins at me.

Nalim rushes to Lemrac and gives him a hug, bandoliers and all.

I'm happy for my new friend. Lemrac is an ally. He'll help Nalim find her father. I don't have to feel responsible for her any more. The thought actually leaves me with a confused feeling of relief, and loss.

"Let's go now and see him!" she's saying eagerly. "Is he in the tunnels, or in one of the safe houses?"

Lemrac shakes his head. "Neither. The WUG have him. He's being held in the interrogation gallow. Nalim, he's not well. He has suffered severe injuries."

She drops his arm and turns away to hide her tears. This is clearly terribly news.

"What are the gallows?" I ask Lemrac quietly while Nalim takes a minute.

"The chop shop where they take dissidents of the WUG," he replies and then looks at Nalim, her back to us, and shakes his head. "She knows no one makes it out of the gallows."

"We have to rescue him!" Nalim says, turning suddenly. "Where are Derrick and CJ? They can set up a distraction and Betsy can rig a bomb!"

"They are all dead," he says gently.

Nalim gasps and turns away again. "Everyone is dead?" she asks, trying to muffle her sobs.

"Except me," he says.

"Why are you still here?" I ask.

"I do not leave Falco behind. While he lives, I bring him water and rats."

"Rats?" asks Nalim.

"There are no food rations anymore in the city. They are starving us now," Lemrac replies as if this is no concern. "So I capture rats. The supply is plentiful."

He shines a flashlight into the corner behind a large furnace to reveal a cage full of live rats. I realize then that Lemrac is either the most loyal friend I've ever met, or completely crazy. Probably both. I like him, and I think we can trust him.

Lemrac turns to Nalim. "We've got to get you to Falco. He must know you are alive before…" Lemrac pauses for a few seconds, "before the battle is over." We know what he's saying. Before Falco dies from his injuries.

They talk privately in low voices so I study the map of Philadelphia pinned to the wall. I think I've found Rake's street, but as I move closer to squint at the street name Lemrac comes up behind me. I try not to flinch. In some ways, he reminds me of the mountain lion – fierce, deadly. "And where are your comrades?" he asks, looking at my map. I point.

"I think they are under the old Marple Toy Factory on Liberty Avenue, but I don't even know for sure," I answer.

Lemrac traces his finger along the tunnel map for a few seconds. He flips a switch on his shotgun and a bright light illuminates the map.

"We can't navigate to that quadrant until sunrise," he announces. "The WUG soldiers are headquartered over there and they won't be gone until morning when the firing lines start back up. You'll never sneak past them tonight. You have to wait.

For now, let's report to Falco."

He reaches into the crate and grabs two gas masks and tosses them to us.

"You'll both need these," he instructs. "WUG patrols bomb the tunnels a few times each day with toxic nerve gas." That explains the burning sensation in my eyes, nose and throat. "When you hear an explosion followed by a loud hissing noise, strap these on and get as low to the ground as you can."

I surrender to the truth that I need Lemrac and Nalim more than they need me. I can't go out alone and try to find London and Rake. There's too much I don't know. I'll be lost or killed down here without their knowledge of how to survive in these tunnels and also their knowledge of WUG positions above. I've never felt so vulnerable before, so dependent on strangers for my survival. I hate it.

But then I remember a time my scoutmaster scolded me for going off on my own during a wilderness trip. I had a dumb accident and slipped on a rock in the stream and knocked myself out. When I came to, hikers were calling for help. I was mad at myself, but Mr. Boar told me, "Son, just because you're good at taking care of yourself doesn't mean you should reject help from strangers when you need it." I guess I was saving up that advice for now.

"Let's go," Lemrac says. The resounding command tone in his voice takes me off guard and I have a moment of panic. When he sees how slow I move in these tunnels will he leave me behind? I scramble to keep up.

Lemrac leads us through what seems like a mile of underground passages, sometimes crossing over and through much larger tunnels and even underground roadways. On several occasions we stop to wait for a passing WUG vehicle before continuing. I take full advantage of the rest to ease my hurting calf. Explosions rattle the ground above. The tunnels are riddled with large chunks of concrete that have shaken loose from the ceiling. The entire tunnel system is extremely dangerous and unpredictable. After about an hour or so of traveling, Lemrac stops at a ladder that leads to one of the storm grates that line the streets above.

"Falco is up here," he says. "This is where the gallows are. You must be very quiet. WUG guards keep a watchful eye."

The sounds coming from the gallows above are horrifying. Screaming, moaning, shooting, and crying are just a few that I can make out among them. At least four languages are being used to shout commands and orders. It sounds like hell on Earth. Lemrac climbs the metal ladder to the storm grate above and makes a few screeching noises that sound exactly like the rats back in the cage. He's calling to Nalim's dad. This is exactly what Dad and Grandpa and I used to do while hunting. We would signal to each other by mimicking birdcalls so as not to alert the other animals to our presence. Lemrac's rats are our birds.

Not long after, a man pulls himself onto the grate. He drags himself across it as if he can't walk. He and Lemrac whisper back and forth, but I can't make out what they are saying. Nalim is staring up at the grate trying to hear. When Lemrac descends the ladder he motions to Nalim. She climbs the ladder as the man reaches through the storm grate to grab her hand. Nalim weeps as he strokes her hair from the unknown hell above. I look away to give her privacy. I'm impressed to see Lemrac masterfully guarding the tunnel from both directions.

At first, no words are spoken between Nalim and her father. They simply touch each other and weep. Then I hear Falco speak, but can't make out what he's saying. I take a few steps closer and Lemrac watches me carefully. Does he mistrust me?

Nalim begins to sob and I hear her whisper, "No, Dad, I can't leave you. We'll fight! We can get you out!"

I hear Falco's raspy voice, "The battle is over, my dearest. There is no more fight left in me. You must leave the city while you still can. I will always be with you."

He presses his face firmly against the grate now, peering into the tunnel beyond Nalim. He grasps something tightly around his neck, but I can't make out what it is.

"Lemrac," he calls in a coarse, commanding tone. "You must leave me. You must take my daughter away from this city. She must not carry my burden. You understand? She must not. It is too dangerous."

"No, Dad," Nalim begs through her tears. "No, I won't leave you!"

"Lemrac," Falco says again. "Take her. I won't lose her to the WUG a second time."

There are shouts from somewhere behind Falco and I hear boots pounding on the concrete above. Lemrac scrambles up the ladder and grabs Nalim around the waist. Falco holds tight to whatever is around his neck. Nalim clings to her father's hand as Lemrac pulls her back down the ladder.

"I love you, Nalim!" cries Falco. "I will always love you!"

I want so badly to help, but I feel utterly helpless. The only thing I can think to do is to take Lemrac's place in the tunnel and keep watch with drawn munti as the big warrior carries a flailing Nalim down the metal ladder.

Standing silhouettes appear over the grate. A soldier slams his gunstock into Falco's back. He coughs with pain and I see blood spatter onto the tunnel wall through the grate. His face crashes against the grate and I can see the whites of his eyes. We make eye contact and he gives me a curious stare before another guard kicks him in the side of the chest as he's dragged away from the grate. Suddenly, shots are fired through the grate and bullets pepper the wall behind me. Bits of concrete spray across my face and nearly get in my eyes.

"Move! Move!" commands Lemrac.

He bursts past me into the dark tunnel with Nalim in tow. Something splashes into the water near my feet. I look down to see what looks like a grenade. Adrenaline pumps into my veins and I sprint after Lemrac. He's running, crouched over, and I hear him counting. Suddenly, he cuts left into a smaller corridor and his arm shoots out and yanks me in front of him and the grenade explodes and rocks the tunnel around me. Fire and rubble blast through the tunnel where we just were. The sound is deafening and for a few seconds after everything goes silent. Then sound returns as a loud ringing in my ears and all I can hear is the pulse of my blood throbbing in my arm and calf. Dizzy and nauseous from the explosion, I follow Lemrac and Nalim turn after turn through the maze of underground tunnels. Finally, we reach the utility room.

It takes several minutes for the ringing to fade. I repack my bandages with the last of the gauze from my first aid kit. Lemrac is busy throwing together supplies from hidden caches in the walls. Nalim sits on the floor with her head in her hands.

"Falco has commanded us to retreat and we must retreat," Lemrac tells us.

"I'm not leaving without my friends." I'm exhausted, again, but I'm so close now. London could be just blocks away! I won't turn back. "You guys go, but I'm not leaving without them. I made a promise and I'm keeping it."

"I made a promise, too," Nalim looks up at me. "I said I'd help you find London, and I will." She turns to Lemrac, who is frowning at this change of plan. "We'll just see if they are alive and then we will go. That's all. We will wait until morning when the WUG move and we'll see if they're still there. It's a simple mission – we sneak in, we sneak out."

Lemrac isn't happy. He slams his shotgun down on the table, looking frustrated. "We cannot attempt it until daybreak," he finally says with a scowl.

I'm too grateful to speak. She's willing to help me find London and Rake even though there's nothing I can do to help her save her father. She'd warned me that people in the city only do things for others because they want something from them, but that was a lie. She's helping me for no other reason than friendship.

I stretch out on the floor and elevate my leg to try to give the calf some relief. Nalim and Lemrac talk quietly in the corner. I have a chance to think about this insane day and my situation. Nalim's words from yesterday (was it just yesterday? It feels like a lifetime ago) haunt me: This is bigger than just you. Don't you get that?

Now I know she's right. The WUG doesn't care about us. We are just a commodity to them, something to exploit. All of their actions are motivated by profit and gain – what's in it for them. So the only way we're ever going to defeat the WUG is if we're not like them. We have to help one another because it's the right thing to do.

We?

I guess I just joined the rebellion.

CHAPTER ELEVEN

We have a few hours to wait. I guess I should be grateful
to grab a few minutes of rest again, but it seems like all we've
been doing is waiting tonight and I just want to get it over with
already. I want to find London and Rake, get them out of this
place and start heading back home.

While we're waiting we share the two cooked pigeons and
a bottle of the maple sap between the three of us. Then Lemrac
uses a piece of charcoal from the fire to trace a path on the map,
showing the route we will travel to Rake and London's location.
I am so excited to hear that it will be no more than an hour's
walk. I study it hard and learn it by heart just in case we are
separated.

Looking at that route sketched in soot, I have a moment of
disbelief. I've really done it! I'm so close to her now, and even
though there is a whole army between me and London, I may
just have a chance at finding her. I don't accept that London
and Rake might be dead already. I reject any reality that says I

made this whole journey for nothing.

I watch as Lemrac reloads a small pile of spent shotgun shells. He carefully replaces the primer, adds in a load of gunpowder and packs the end with whatever he can find. Some loads include little rocks, nails, nuts and bolts, pieces of metal. He gladly accepts the lead balls I brought along to use with my slingshot. He carefully pours melted candle wax in to cap the top. I make three special rounds for him that I call Purple Death, filling the empty shells with shards of glass drizzled with lethal monkshood jelly. He seals the tops of those with melted wax too. While we're waiting around, I use some of the candle wax to seal and waterproof the seams around the soles of my moccasins. This will make for quieter and more comfortable travel through the tunnels.

Lemrac teaches Nalim and I the rat-call signals that he and Falco use to communicate in code through the tunnels. There are rat calls for YES, NO, STOP, CONTINUE, LEAVE ME, COME TO ME, ATTACK and RETREAT. Nalim and I practice with each other until we know them by heart.

I use a length of 550 paracord from my bug-out bag to weave a bandoleer of my own that holds ten munti across my chest for faster reloading. I tie a small plastic bottle around my neck and fill it with monkshood jelly so that I don't have to mess with the bulky glass jelly jar while navigating the dark tunnels. With this new rig I can pull a munti, dip it and load it in less than two seconds.

Nalim spends several minutes sharpening all of our knives on a broken piece of porcelain toilet she scavenged from the tunnels. By the time she's finished, our knives are shaving sharp. She uses her knife to carve the tips of her .22 rounds into hollow points for more lethal impact. Her hair is pulled back in a tight bun and she's mimicked Lemrac's diagonal war paint design on her face with black ash from the fire. She looks quite different from how she looked at dinner on her birthday with the butterfly hair clip pinning her bangs back. I like both versions of Nalim. In fact, the more I get to know Nalim, the more I find to like about her.

"Aren't you scared?" I ask her when Lemrac goes into the tunnels to relieve himself.

"Of what?"

"Dying, I guess."

"You've got to have something to lose to be afraid of dying." She sounds so bleak and I don't know how to respond.

Finally, I say, "Well, I don't want to lose you."

Nalim smiles and I know I've said the right thing.

When Lemrac comes back he reaches into the rat cage and, one by one, grabs four rats by the tale and cracks their heads against the wall to kill them quickly. After masterfully skinning them, he fries all four on a hobo-can stove in the corner and offers us each one. Although I know I shouldn't turn down food, I decline.

I want to get out of these tunnels before I resort to eating rats. It's the principle of the matter, not the rats.

"Lemrac, what did my father mean when he said he doesn't want me to carry his burden?"

Lemrac sighs deeply and stares in the flames of his small hobo stove.

"Falco carries a heavy burden in our fight against the WUG," he finally replies. "He is one of a very select few who carries the burden. Only he knows what it is and what to do with it."

I can tell it's not the answer Nalim is looking for, and I don't blame her because it's not much of an answer at all. She drops her head into her hands and sighs. I can't imagine what it must feel like for her to abandon her father in the gallows, knowing that he's still alive.

I know what it's like to lose a father. I begged Dad not to go back to Asia when he was home the last time.

"Omaha," he said, staring blankly into the woods, "I've started something that I must finish with the Gi-Nong. The right decision isn't always the easy decision. Sometimes, doing what you know you must do can be the hardest choice of all."

I understand those words now more than ever. The last place on earth I want to be right now is in these godforsaken wretched tunnels beneath Philadelphia, but I know I must be here in order to save London.

I reach into the front pocket of my bug out bag and pull out Dad's Eagle Scout patch. Even though I didn't earn my own, there's something about his that gives me comfort. It's symbolic of the good in people. I trace my finger across the banner on the patch, which reads BE PREPARED in bold, royal blue letters. I guess I'm about to find out if I'm really prepared to face what's coming.

***

We rest in shifts. I'm too keyed up to sleep. I walk into the connecting tunnel every few minutes and peer through the storm grate to try to see the sky and get an estimate of what time it is. Lemrac tells us it's time to go when it's around three in the morning. Finally! I can't wait to get moving. We set off on our trek to Rake's apartment building on Liberty Avenue.

Lemrac has a flashlight with a red lens cover. It's much less noticeable from above and also allows our eyes to adjust back to complete darkness more quickly if he suddenly has to shut it off. He has warned us that we must travel in complete silence so that we can hear all other activity in the tunnel and be proactive rather than reactive when the WUG strike. I note that he says "when," not "if."

We've been walking for fifteen minutes and we're just passing an entrance into one of the larger tunnels when I smell the distinct odor of cigarette smoke. I immediately sound the rat signal for STOP. Lemrac turns to me and I motion as if smoking a cigarette. He flips his red headlamp off just as three WUG guards turn the corner into our tunnel. They are only thirty yards ahead and automatic rifles are in their hands and they are coming toward us. If they were wearing night-vision goggles, we'd be dead by now, but they only have headlamps and they can't see beyond the beam of their lights. Nalim and I silently slip into a corridor on the right side of the tunnel and Lemrac disappears into one on the opposite side.

I know Lemrac already has Purple Death loaded in his shotgun, and I silently ready a dipped munti.

The soldiers' lights brighten the tunnel as the splashing of their steps becomes louder and louder. They have become far too complacent in their patrol of the tunnels, especially on this day. Leaving them no time to react, Lemrac sends two rounds of Purple Death down the narrow tunnel. There is a high-pitched shatter of glass against concrete and then screams of agony. The other, now-familiar sounds of monkshood toxins coursing through the body soon follow and then there is silence in the tunnel once again.

"Impressive poison!" Lemrac whispers to me in an almost giddy tone.

I take the lead and ten minutes later silently dispatch three more WUG soldiers with dipped munti. Lemrac is clearly delighted by the silence, simplicity and effectiveness of my Gi-Nong slingshot. He can't resist the urge to ask about it when we stop for a quick break in one of the rebels' secret utility rooms along the way.

"From where did you source that weapon?"

"My father fought against Gi-Nong warriors in the jungles of Asia. This belonged to one that he killed."

"I have seen these Gi-Nong," Lemrac says soberly. "The General brought them here as slaves to carry out his orders."

I can't believe what I'm hearing. The Gi-Nong are here! Despite myself, I feel a shiver of foreboding. Dad always said they were the toughest warriors he'd ever met. "Fearless ought to be their motto," I once overheard him telling Grandpa.

"What are they doing here?" I ask Lemrac. I notice I'm gripping my slingshot tightly and relax my hand.

"After the General destroyed the Gi-Nong homeland, he put their women and children into work camps and gave the men a choice: work for the WUG, or never see their families again." Lemrac gives a small shrug with his massive shoulders. "The General is no fool. He knows the Gi-Nong are expert trackers and ruthless killers. He has been using them here in the city to carry out his orders."

The Gi-Nong killed my father and now they work for the WUG. I killed a man for the first time only three days ago, but right now I feel very willing to kill a few more, especially if they are Gi-Nong.

"At first Falco thought maybe they could be allies, yes? They hate the WUG as we do. Falco tried to earn their trust and build an alliance but the Gi-Nong trust no one except Gi-Nong. Falco says we have a chance if we can partner with Gi-Nong because they work side-by-side with the WUG, but now there is no hope."

I will never forgive the Gi-Nong for killing my father, but even I can feel some sympathy for the situation they're in. They don't have a homeland anymore, and their women and children are hostages to the WUG. That means their women and children are probably dead.

My neck flushes with heat at the thought of Gi-Nong warriors being here in Philadelphia. I draw my fingers through a black, oily residue on the door of the utility furnace. In the faint reflection from a broken window I paint my face with symbols of my ancestors. Eagle wings across my eyes will give me keen vision in battle. A mountain lion track on my left cheek represents the strength and force I will need to overcome my enemy. The viper on my right cheek imitates the death strikes I will make with my slingshot. I slice my hand and drip a fresh red line of blood down the center of my face to symbolize the blood drawn from my father by the Gi-Nong.

Nalim and Lemrac watch me in silence and Lemrac gives a slight nod of approval. Nalim dips her hand in the black sludge and draws three slashes across each cheek. We stare at each other, my brown eyes into her blue eyes, and I feel our hearts pounding to the same rhythm. If it is war they want, it is war they'll get.

***

We're on the move again, and I ignore the pain of my body. It's time, and my whole focus is on completing my mission. In darkness, we arrive at the tunnel beneath Liberty Avenue. As we planned earlier, Lemrac and Nalim stay behind while I climb up through a storm drain on my own. It's too risky for a group of three to be roaming above ground. I'm traveling light, carrying only my machete, slingshot and munti, headlamp, binoculars and map of the city. Carefully, I creep onto the still, dark street – or, rather, what is left of the street. There is rubble piled up everywhere, which gives me places to hide as I watch obsessively for snipers in the tall buildings on either side of me. I count three cars on fire – one just a blackened frame still smoldering. The air stinks of rotting garbage and noxious chemicals. Dead bodies lie in careless heaps, their arms and legs and necks twisted into broken poses, which makes my bile rise. I feel as bleak as the landscape. My chances of finding London and Rake alive now seem ridiculously minuscule. No one is meant to survive this destruction.

I dart from one heap of rubble to the next, zigzagging toward my destination. I can see a faded red sign hanging haphazardly off the side of a building: MARPLE TOY FACTORY LUXURY APARTMENTS. They don't look very luxurious today, I think. There isn't a window left unbroken on the ten-story building, and soot on the outside lets me know there was a fire. How recently, I can't tell. The knot tightens in the pit of my stomach. This building feels completely deserted, but I have to check.

I slip inside the doorless front foyer just as bullet shots ring out in an endless rat-a-tat of machine gun fire. Lemrac has told me the WUG and Gi-Nong slaves start the firing lines every day at sunrise. I can't spare it a thought. My eyes scan the terrain: a long hallway, every door smashed off its hinges, walls riddled with bullet holes. A message has been spray painted across the wall of the hallway: "GELOSCHT 5-3." I remember that loschen means 'to clear' in German. If I'm correct, it seems the WUG cleared this building yesterday.

I check the exit diagram on the wall and locate the stairwell in the back of the lobby. I silently move down the stairs into a concrete-floored basement. It is dark and dank, and I see chain-link storage spaces lining the walls. It is just as Rake described. I'm here. This is it! I've never been so nervous in my life. My heart pounds with fear and excitement. Is London close by? Cautiously, I click on my headlamp. A row of washing machines is at attention against the far wall. Except for some dripping water pipes, the basement is completely silent.

"London?" I whisper into the room. "Rake?"

Silence answers me.

I move to the first storage closet and look inside. There is a bicycle and boxes of papers. The space next to it has only a few old plastic bags and papers. The third space is occupied by rats that scatter when I make a hissing noise. They've been feeding on the body of a middle-aged man who wears a t-shirt that reads "I'd rather be fishing." An array of fishing poles, nets and tackle boxes crowd the space around him. There's a picture tacked to the wall of him and a young boy holding up a big stringer of blue gill at the edge of a pond somewhere. I wonder if that's his son. There is no blood in the storage locker, and I see the empty pill bottle still clasped in his hands. I've seen so much death in the last few days, but I still fight back tears. All this senseless death – all this suffering – it's so wrong. I hate the WUG, the Gi-Nong and, now, The General.

As I approach the fourth storage unit, I stop breathing, because someone has painted a small red rose in the upper left corner of the door. Rosa rugosa. Rake left me a message! The unit is empty, but there is a small air vent toward the bottom of the back wall.

"London?" I whisper into the grate. "Rake? It's me, Omaha!"

No one answers. They might be unconscious. They might

be starving. I take my machete and frantically start hacking out
a hole in the sheetrock wall.

"I'm here! I'm here!" I say over and over.

When the hole is finally big enough, I shine my light inside
and the first thing I see is that no one is there. A rust-colored
blanket is crumpled against the back of the small crawl space.
I recognize the color as old blood. There are some rags, t-shirts
and a scarf of the same color.

"Bandages," I think. Someone was wounded. Light is
coming from the other side of the crawl space and I see with
a chill that an air vent was ripped out of the wall. The WUG
found them in here, and took them.

I shove through the hole I've made and land on something
soft. I shine my headlamp down and see a leather backpack.
I know immediately that it's London's. I would recognize her
distinctive hand stitching anywhere. It's the same as on my
sheath and moccasins.

She was here! She was in this room waiting for me, but I am
too late. The enormity of this truth hits me like a punch to my
solar plexus and I fold up and moan. I took too long. I failed to
protect her. The WUG came for her and I wasn't here.

I press my face into the backpack and sob uncontrollably.
I've held in my emotions this entire journey, but now I'm
undone. I shake the backpack as if trying to make it confess
something to me.

"Where is she?" I demand. "Where is she!?"

All my energy drains away. I might never get up off this
floor. What's the point? I lost London. I failed.

My hand feels something papery on the floor and I pick it
up to look. It's a 5x7 photo Mom took of London and me in
the meadow when we were about 13. I mailed it to London on

Easter last year.

I remember everything about that day. I close my eyes and feel the sun on my face, smell the breeze coming through the pine valley below. I hear the sounds of the meadow and London laughing and teasing me.

I loved her in a way I will never love anyone else, and now she's gone forever. The WUG took her from me. The General has stolen her from my future.

I decide right then that I will not be leaving this city. Mom and Macy will have to make do on their own. Macy knows how to hunt; they have their garden and they have each other. I will protect them the only way I really can: by finishing the war the WUG and this General are waging against my family. I will stealthily kill every last WUG soldier in this city and will not stop until I am face to face with The General who gives them orders. The deaths of London and Rake and all the other innocents who have been killed will be avenged.

I'm putting the photo in my pocket when I notice there is writing on the back. I wipe the tears from my eyes and take a closer look. I didn't write anything on it when I mailed it to her. These words are in London's handwriting:

Omaha – If you find this photo then you already know that we've been taken. Rake is badly wounded. He wants you to know that he has done the best he could to protect me. The General has ordered WUG soldiers to round up people in the square for interrogations. There's nowhere else to hide and I can hear their dogs getting closer and I'm afraid they'll find us now. I should have come home months ago. I love you Omaha. I always have. I will wait for you in Heaven's Great Meadow. Love, London

How long ago did she write this? I grab one of the rags and feel dampness underneath the crusty dried blood. They were taken just a few hours ago! That means there's still a chance she's alive.

I grab London's backpack and race upstairs. I don't need to consult a map – I can follow the sounds of gunfire, which shatter the eerie silence of this empty city. I'm driven by desperation. Any one of those shots I'm hearing could be tearing through London! Like a field mouse in the meadow I scurry from one tuft of cover to the next. In less than a minute I'm crouched behind a dumpster, the city square ahead. A chain link fence topped with razor wire and heavily guarded by WUG soldiers borders it. All the soldiers are facing the square, their backs to me. I am tempted to take them all down and watch them fall like dominoes, but I have to get London out first.

I need height to see what's happening, so I free climb to the top of the dumpster and lay flat. A squad of men herd a group of five terrified, wailing people to stand in front of a large concrete wall that was once a handball court.

"You are traitor of World Union Government," an officer screams through a megaphone in broken English. "You punish by death."

Shots ring out, then the bodies are dragged away by the Gi-Nong slaves and thrown into waiting dump trucks. The whole process is then repeated.

I slip down and back up slowly until I'm at the doorway of a tall building that looks down on the square. I fly up the stairs to the tenth floor, not even feeling the pain in my calf. I'm charged with adrenaline. At the blown-out window I stay low and glass the square below with my binoculars. Two hundred people are penned in, waiting to be marched up in groups of five and shot. My binoculars shift from prisoner to prisoner, searching for London. Please God let her be here. I search every face, but I don't see London's and I don't know what Rake looks like. My heart sinks.

I move down the hallway into what was once an office, looking for a window with a different view of the square where maybe I can get a better look at the people crowded in the back. I step silently over smashed cubicle dividers and fallen steel beams when I suddenly hear a silenced rifle shot to my left. Dad used to have a silenced rifle and I would recognize that sound anywhere. I freeze and hear the gun being reloaded. I strain my eyes in the dim light and see a WUG sniper poised at the open window, selectively shooting helpless prisoners who wander too close to the fence bordering the square.

Every muscle in my body tenses. In the dim light I watch as he takes another silent, calculated shot. The minute he does, I leap toward him, my machete out. He spins the unloaded rifle toward me and I whip my machete at his chest, just as I've practiced hundreds of times before in the oak stump that remains in our front yard. The impact knocks him from his seat and onto the floor, shock and fear on his face. Before he can break radio silence my knees pin his arms. As he gurgles helplessly, drowning in his own blood, I lean in close so he can hear me.

"Death to the WUG," I whisper. I hold him while he shakes with death throes. I don't look away. Part of me wonders if I've cracked. I'm killing a man, and I want to watch, want to feel the life drain out of him. Who am I becoming?

Time seems to slow down as the man dies beneath me. I flash back to a moment with Grandpa. We had hiked deep into the woods for two days to harvest pecans from a small, forgotten grove. It was a long and arduous hike just to gather nuts, but Mom loved them so much and being in the woods together was our joy, so we hiked there year after year. Just before he died, Grandpa disappeared for two days. When he came back, he was carrying a small pecan sapling from that grove. He planted it in the front yard, right in front of Mom's kitchen window.

"Omaha, I'll be long gone before pecans ever grow on this tree," Grandpa said as I watched him place the tree in the hole I dug for him. "I'll never be able to harvest the fruit of this tree, but you and your children will enjoy these pecans for many years beyond my life. My reward is knowing that I've done something today that will benefit the future generations of my family."

High above the square where innocents are being systematically slaughtered, I killed one of the men responsible. I don't feel remorse; I feel righteous, because now I understand Grandpa's lesson. There's no more standing by and just reacting or hiding. It will take every one of us to defeat the WUG, and that mission has to be my mission. It's bigger than just rescuing London and Rake. Nalim was right: if the WUG remain in power, there is no future for any of us.

I feel no remorse as I take the sniper's position at the window and scan the square below with my binoculars. Still no London. But now I can see snipers in the other buildings around the square, who are dropping prisoners when they venture too close to the fences. Every few minutes a new truck of prisoners is delivered through a heavily fortified gate. Armed guards round up another group of five prisoners and march them to the wall. The WUG International Allegiance Song starts to play through a loudspeaker above the square, almost drowning out the sounds of crying and screaming prisoners.

This window has a much clearer view of the holding pen. I scan faces for what seems like eternity. I methodically work my way from right to left, making sure I get a good look at each prisoner's face. Huge planters of flowers are positioned in a pattern throughout the large open space. Once, this Philadelphia square was probably a pretty place where people ate lunch when the weather was warm and enjoyed the blooming roses. The roses are just starting to bloom and for a moment I train my binoculars on them. Mom grows many of these same varieties in the garden at home, and I have a strange moment of homesickness. There aren't just roses, I see. One planter is filled with bright yellow daffodils, Macy's favorite flower. Another planter towers with orange day lilies. Though they won't bloom until later this summer, I'd recognize them anywhere. We feast on the tubers of the orange day lily each spring and Mom makes amazing fried fritters out of the orange blooms in July. It is one of my favorite wild edibles. London and I used to spend hours gathering them together. And hundreds of brightly colored tulips shoot like fireworks from the top of a circular raised planter in the middle of the square and remind me of the wildflowers that pepper the green meadow leading to my pine valley. A brilliant, white–bloomed, carpet-like creeper drapes over the edges of a diamond-shaped planter in the corner and looks just like the heavy snow drifts that collect on the barn roof at home every winter.

The largest display of roses I've ever seen grows in another diamond-shaped planter. It's at least twenty feet wide. The tightly clenched crimson buds are preparing to burst open in just a few weeks. They remind me of the Rosa Rugosa patch at home with its dense thicket of thorns and brambles. Was it only five days ago that I carved that discrete path to the entrance of the bunker?

Omaha, focus! I tell myself sternly.

My eyes suddenly catch something out-of-place amongst the rose bushes. In the mulch at the base of the plants I see a few day lily stems. That's odd, because the orange day lily planter is on the opposite side of the square. A few feet into the bushes there are a few more, with leaves this time, and then a couple more even farther toward the center. Were rats or other rodents dragging them over there for food? My eyes strain to see clearly in the dim morning light as I follow the subtle trail of day lily stems and leaves into the thorny maze of brambles.

I focus the lens on my binoculars to make sure my eyes aren't playing tricks on me. Is that the silhouette of a person hiding inside? I move to another window and get a better angle and my heart speeds up. I would know this silhouette anywhere. I've seen it many times against the sun in the meadow at home. I see it when I close my eyes each evening, and in the dreams that haunt my days and nights.

It's London. She's taken refuge in the labyrinth of rugosa. She's alive!

CHAPTER TWELVE

London is alive. I'm simultaneously weak with relief, and filled with renewed hope. All I need to do is figure out how to get her out of the rosebush planter and into the tunnels. I scan all around her position and then take out my map and start making notes. There is a manhole cover twenty feet in front of the planter. If I can find my way through the tunnels to that location, then I can find a way to get her out and she can escape underground with me.

First, I have to take out the snipers who will be able to spot her the minute she leaves the rose thicket. Luckily, there is a WUG vehicle parked on one side of it, which will provide cover from the snipers I assume the WUG have positioned on the opposite side of the square. But London will be completely exposed to the snipers on this side. I scan the buildings to the left and right of me with the binoculars and locate two snipers. They aren't even bothering to hide themselves.

I reposition the dead soldier's shooting tripod and pry

the heavy sniper rifle from under his lifeless body. I find the
ammunition in his pocket and reload. Then I take careful aim
at the sniper to my left and silently blow him back into the
darkness of the room where he sits. I can't get a good angle on
the sniper in the building to my right so I have to move up one
floor and several rooms over. This window still has glass, but
it's the kind that opens, so I crack it only enough to slip out
the gun barrel and carefully take aim. To my surprise, his rifle
is pointed at my building, at the window where I was a few
moments ago. He is panning my building, using his scope as
binoculars to try to figure out what's wrong. Just as his scope
points directly at my cracked window I pull the trigger and send
a silent round through his chest. It's an immediate lights out for
him.

Threats from above on this side of the square are now
cleared, but it won't be long until other soldiers figure out that
something is amiss. Someone will sound an alarm and more
soldiers will pour in to investigate.

I rush back down the stairs and slip into a manhole just
outside the building. I try to keep all my weight on my good
leg as I climb down the rebar ladder, but it's awkward. I catch
my breath at the bottom and take a moment to recall the tunnel
map that I memorized. I'm not precisely sure where I am, but I
have to trust my gut. I move as fast and as silently as I can, alert
to the possibility of running into WUG patrols and hoping for
some familiar sign to tell me that I'm on the right track.

An arm reaches out and yanks me to the side of the tunnel
and a meaty hand clamps down over my mouth.

"Where have you been?" Lemrac says in a shouting whisper.

"Mmmff!" I try to answer. He removes his hand. "I found
her! She's close!"

"You were gone so long we thought you were captured." Nalim's face is drawn with worry.

"I found her," I say again. "But she's trapped in the square where they've got a firing line. She's hiding in the middle of the rose bushes. But I have a plan. We can get her out!" I tell them about the snipers and the manhole and how I think we can do it.

"From the lion's den to the hornet's nest – I like these odds," says Lemrac, tightening the laces on his combat boots.

"How will she know what to do?" Nalim asks doubtfully. "The whole plan hinges on her moving when it's time, but she doesn't even know you're here."

I'd thought of that already. "I know I can get her attention. There's a storm grate on a curb that faces the bushes. I can send her a message. But we need to move now. I killed three WUG snipers to give us a window of cover, but it won't be long until someone finds them and starts looking for us."

Nalim and Lemrac are ready to join me even though it may well be a suicide mission. I'm suddenly moved by their friendship, even though I know they are fighting for something bigger than London and me. They are fighting for what they believe is right.

"You don't have to go with me," I say. "If you want to turn back, I understand and wouldn't blame you. This isn't your fight anymore."

"And miss the opportunity to kill more WUG scum, are you kidding me?" replies Lemrac.

"I'm not leaving you, either, Omaha," says Nalim with a tight smile. "We're in this together, right?"

"Right," I say. "Together."

She squeezes my hand.

"This will always be my fight," she adds. "Not just today and not just for you. Now let's go kill some WUG. I'm sick of waiting around."

I show Lemrac the location on my map and he darts off fearlessly into the dark tunnel ahead. Nalim and I jog along behind him, which makes my calf throb painfully. I struggle to keep up. Suddenly, the loud squeal of a siren blasts from the street above. I hear the sound of a manhole cover being lifted and dropped back down in the distance. A shrill, hissing noise quickly follows.

"Masks! Masks!" orders Lemrac.

A flash of light and piercing explosion fills the cramped tunnel with a dense green fog. Immediately, my eyes fill with water and my lungs cramp with pain. I instinctively pull the gas mask from around my neck up over my face like we practiced and take a deep breath of filtered air. I feel instant relief in my aching lungs. I hear a muffled scream behind me and turn to find Nalim clawing at the mask on her face.

"It's not working! It's not working," screams Nalim from inside the mask.

I can see her eyes are bloodshot and she starts to cough. Before I can react, Lemrac pushes me aside. In a skilled, smooth motion he whips the mask off Nalim's face and replaces it with his own. I can tell by her deep breaths that his mask is working. Lemrac puts on Nalim's mask and starts to shake violently. The mask is defective.

We lock eyes. There's nowhere to run, and there are no more masks. Suddenly, Lemrac is lunging for a manhole cover above.

"Run!" he screams back at me with a raw voice. He bursts out of the manhole and grabs his gun and I hear him blasting away. I know I should run, but I can't just leave him. I start to climb out and I'm halfway up when Nalim grabs me and shakes her head vehemently.

"We can't just leave him!" My voice is muffled through the mask.

We watch as Lemrac, muscles gleaming in the morning light, steam from his breath climbing high into the cool morning air above, takes on the WUG alone.

"I fight for Falco!" he screams, blasting away. "I die for Falco!"

He's giving up his own life without a second thought to save Nalim. It is the most heroic thing I've ever witnessed. He gives everything in his power for what he believes, and his sense of honor and duty to Falco and the fight against the WUG are stronger than his love of his own life. I can't help but think that we all might be asked to give everything today.

Nalim tries to pull me away, but I must watch. His shotgun is no match for WUG machine guns and explosives. A bullet tears through his left leg and blood sprays through the open manhole as he crashes to one knee. He sees me and is furious.

"RUUUUNNNNN!!!!"

Nalim and I grab each other's hands and run.

The nerve gas dissipates quickly through the storm grates above. I tentatively test the air and it's clear by the time we reach the square.

Nalim removes her mask. "Lemrac died for me," she sobs.

Dnoces Tnemdnema. Lemrac believed Nalim was worth fighting for, and dying for. So do I.

"You're worth dying for," I say. "And he died the way he wanted: taking down the WUG. It was a good death." I hear myself say it and then I wonder what that means. Is any death a good death? I think about the sniper who died half an hour ago by my hand. He breathed his last breath while I held him pinned to the floor. Grandpa and Dad taught me to be a hunter, but the WUG and their war have made me a warrior. Both involve killing, but they are not the same. I'm proud of my hunting skills, but I'm never glad when the animal dies, because I respect its life. I can't say I've felt that way about the WUG soldiers I've killed, or about Fink. I was glad they died, and glad I killed them. Like Nalim and Lemrac, I want to kill The General. So what does that say about me? I wish Dad were here so I could talk to him about it. I get the sense that he grappled with these questions himself when he was fighting the Gi-Nong.

I know I'll think more about this later. But right now, London is waiting just a few yards away. I can hardly believe it's finally happening! I am getting her out.

I climb the narrow rebar ladder to the storm grate. The rosebush planter is right across the street. It's impossible to see inside from this angle. I pull the photo of London that I found in the wall cavity from my front pocket and roll it into a small tube, which I then fold in half. I drape it over the band of my slingshot and silently launch it into the center of the rose thicket. It disappears into the darkness.

Did she see it? I haven't got anything else I can shoot in there that she'd recognize.

I wait nervously and finally I see a face peek out. It's her! The truth of her being alive takes my breath away. I make a very subtle rat call to get her attention. She looks around to see where the sound is coming from. I make it again and finally she turns my way. When she sees me, her hand covers her mouth as if to stifle a gasp. Tears fill her eyes.

London is alive and she knows I've come for her! She knows

I've kept my promise against all odds. She's knows I've not abandoned her.

Beneath me in the tunnels, Nalim makes an impatient rat call for WHAT IS HAPPENING?

I reply WAIT and signal London to notice the manhole cover across the street from her planter. She nods with understanding and disappears back into the rose hedge. She reappears about thirty seconds later with someone behind her. I can only assume he is Rake. I motion them to wait a second and disappear back down into the tunnel.

"There are two of them," I say to Nalim. "I'm going to slide open the manhole cover and bring them in. Get your mask ready just in case. You might have to run. Do you know how to get out of here?"

"Yes," she replies calmly. "All of the tunnels are marked."

"Good," I reply. "I'll be back."

"Omaha?"

I stop and look at her. Nalim pauses for second as if changing her mind about what she's about to say, but then she nods once. "Go save her," she says, and then she looks away from me and busies herself loading shotgun rounds into her gun from one of the bandoleers that crosses her chest. I want to say more to her, but I don't have the words and there's no time for more conversation.

I climb the ladder to the manhole and slowly slide the heavy metal cover a few inches to peek through. I see London and Rake waiting just inside the rose bushes. I give a small wave of my fingers and start opening the cover wider as London hops down out of the planter and helps Rake behind her. This is the first time I've ever seen Rake and he looks quite different than I had imagined from our many conversations on the subnet. A yellow bandanna holds back shaggy red hair. He wears a pair of large, green-tinted goggles and is shorter than I am by half a foot. His pale white face shines like a beacon against the dark rose bush camouflage.

London has to help him because his leg is badly wounded and he can't walk by himself. He clings to her, and she stumbles a few steps forward and then casts a panicked look in my direction. In a flash I remember how Lemrac didn't hesitate when he saw that Nalim was in trouble. I drop my bug-out bag down to Nalim and pull myself up with a leap. In five steps I'm at their side, grabbing Rake in a fireman's carry.

"It's about time you showed up Reuben," he rasps.

There's nothing funny about the situation, but I'm grinning even as bullets pierce through the WUG vehicle shielding us from the snipers on the opposite side of the square. The three of us duck behind one of the huge tires. Time seems to stand still. I look into London's familiar brown eyes and see her amazement and gratitude – and something else that I've never seen before in her expression when she's looked at me. She's not looking at me like a brother. Never in my life has so much been said without speaking. Her dark brown hair is pulled back into a long pony tail that's tightly wrapped in long leather strips. A fur scarf made from patches of fox, raccoon and elk drapes around her neck and shoulders, and an intricate brown leather harness is strapped over her shoulders and across her chest. She, too, has filled out in the two short years that have felt like a lifetime. She left a girl, but now I'm gazing at a woman.

"Omaha," she breathes, and I want to wrap her in my arms right there, but a bullet whizzes by and I'm brought back to reality.

"I'll be right behind you," I promise. "Go!"

She gives me one last look and then sprints for the manhole. Nalim's hands shoot up to help guide her down the ladder.

"Come on, Rake, it's our turn," I say.

"I'm just waiting on you," he replies.

He looks scared, but I don't have time to reassure him. I hoist him over my shoulder in a fireman's carry and pray my leg will support us both. Then I leap into the street and dash toward the manhole. I ignore the pain and the bullets I imagine shooting toward us and focus on closing the distance. We're only two feet away when a soldier tackles me from my left side. The three of us crash to the ground. I grapple with the soldier, trying to reach my machete. Rake is crawling for the last few feet to the manhole.

"Go!" I scream, trying to fight free from the soldier's arm around my chest and pushing Rake with my feet to get him closer to where Nalim and London wait for us.

This is not the way I imagined it would be. It's all happening so fast. But as long as she survives – that's all that matters now.

"RUN, NALIM!" I scream as loud as I can until the soldiers choking grip around my neck cut off the air. I frantically pull on my machete but it's not coming free of the sheath. I hear two close gun shots and blood suddenly spatters across my chest. Am I hit? The WUG soldier is suddenly dead weight on top of me. I see Nalim duck back into the manhole holding the .22 revolver and I use my last strength to shove the soldier off of me so I can follow.

But it's no use. A squad has me in their range now and their guns are up and pointing at me. One of the soldiers runs right at me and pulls a grenade from a pouch on the front of his vest. He cocks his arm to throw it into the manhole. Time slows down; I see his arm going back as I finally am able to yank the machete from my side. I fling it at him with the force of lighting. He pulls the pin just as the blade slams through his chest and sends him flying backward. The live grenade flies through the air and lands between me and the hole. I roll away from it toward the WUG truck. There's no chance to cover my ears before the grenade explodes.

The blast rips through my head and concusses every part of my body. The blast picks me up and throws me into the concrete base of the rosebush planter. The last thought I have before everything goes black is that London, Rake and Nalim have to survive. They have to.

CHAPTER THIRTEEN

I'm unconscious, and then I'm awake and drowning in icy water. My lungs burn with the need for oxygen and I uncontrollably breathe in freezing cold water. The pressure in my chest is unreal and I'm panicking trying to get to the surface. Something is holding me under. I start to black out again and suddenly my head is yanked backward and I'm coughing out water while gasping for air. Before I can take a full breath, someone pushes my head back into the water and I can't stop the urge to inhale. Freezing water fills my lungs and once again I'm drowning. I struggle against the hand holding me under, and finally it yanks my head back out. Grateful, I cough out water and gasp for breath. Then I'm plunged back in.

By the fourth time I give up. I don't have the strength to fight. That's when the pressure on my head releases and I can lift my own head out of the basin of icy water and cough up my lungs. The pain in my chest can be ignored because of the simple pleasure of being alive and breathing air. I take a full minute to deeply appreciate this act that I've taken for granted my whole life, and while I'm at it I take stock of my situation. My hands are bound behind my back. The gunshot wound in my arm hurts, but no worse than usual. My calf is raw, but I can bear it. My ribs are sore, maybe broken.

Without warning, my head is thrust back into the cold water. The hand at the back of my head carelessly slams my forehead onto the far edge of the metal container and a sharp pain shoots like electricity across my scalp. The water instantly turns red as the gash on my forehead gushes blood.

I have random thoughts while I bleed out into the water in which I'm drowning. I think about how some people freak out at the sight of their own blood. Macy is like that. My little sister gets nauseous when she nicks herself with a blade. I don't. I get angry. Seeing my own blood incites a feeling of rage, particularly when someone else is drawing it. It happens right now, even though I'm helpless and drowning. A surge of rage goes through me and I struggle with all of my might against the hand that's trying to kill me. A swift kick to the side of my chest knocks out the little bit of air that's left in my lungs. I again draw in water and choke uncontrollably. Just as I start to black out again I'm thrown onto the concrete floor. I cough and vomit up water. My lungs have never burned like this in my life. I'm dizzy and my ears are ringing. Blood drips from the gash in my forehead, fills my left eye, but it doesn't take perfect vision to see that I'm in a large, dimly lit room. I am on the floor next to a metal chair and a small table with what I assume are tools of torture on a rusty tray. As I quickly scan the room, this is but one of what seems to be six of these stations, all equally spaced in a circle around the water tank, which is now a murky maroon color from my blood.

Each chair is occupied with a prisoner, all in different stages of torture and interrogations. I try as quickly as I can to survey each one to make sure Nalim, London or Rake are not among them. Please God let them not be in here. A lifeless body with a black bag over the head is tied to the chair directly across the water tank at 12 o'clock. I can't tell if they are alive or if it's one of my friends. Next to them at 2 o'clock is a man so badly beaten I can barely recognize the features of his grossly swollen face. I can tell by the color of his hair that it's not Rake. At 4 o'clock sits a man whose face is not harmed but his hands are duct taped to the metal chair arms and each of his fingers are badly broken and dislocated. His eyes are closed as he silently takes slow long breaths. I dislocated my index finger while carrying a ladder once on the farm and the pain was excruciating until Grandpa popped it back into place. I can't imagine the pain the man at 4 o'clock must be suffering. I am at 6 o'clock, slumped in a heap at the base of my chair. 8 o'clock is a woman who appears to be in her 40s. Her head is shaved and her face shows great concern as we make eye contact. She is restrained with what appears to be clear plastic wrap to the chair arms and legs.

"He's too young," she screams, looking toward the dark back corner of the room where stands the silhouette of someone in the shadows just outside of the light. The WUG guard at her station guard quickly comes from behind and stretches the plastic wrap around her mouth, which prevents her from saying anything else. She struggles in the chair but it has no effect on the restraints and I can't make out what she's saying any longer.

Two guards step from behind and roughly hoist me by the arms into the chair at my torture station. Still struggling to catch a breath, I glance at the 10 o'clock position. It's Falco!

He's alive, but badly injured. I can see him clearly, unlike yesterday through the storm drain. He's tall, I'd estimate over six feet, and lean with muscle. His long grey hair is receding but he doesn't look old. A thick salt and pepper beard gives him a distinguished look, even after what he's been through in recent days. I can immediately see how he could be a great leader. He's tied at the waist around the chair and slumped over. His right leg is clearly broken at the knee. His shirt is torn and ragged at the back and covered in blood. I assume this is from some sort of previous whipping in the gallows where I last saw him. Blood pools on the ground beneath him. His eyes are open and they widen when we make eye contact. He recognizes me from the tunnel! He says something but my ears are still ringing and I can't make it out. I want to tell him Nalim is alive but I stop myself. Is she alive? I don't even know for sure. Did they escape after the grenade exploded?

I count several WUG guards in their olive-drab uniforms spaced in no particular order throughout the room. Four other men are lined up against the wall–small, wiry, brown-skinned, they wear plain brown coveralls. Their faces are tattooed in spirals and lines, and small animal bones jut out of their pierced noses. I recognize them with a chill. These are the Gi-Nong.

I'm nearly dead and every inch of my body hurts, but I want to lunge at these savages and tear their throats out. As I start to struggle, my wrists and ankles are roughly shackled to the chair with cold steel chains.

As my mind races, a tall, gaunt, shallow-faced WUG officer steps into the light from the dark corner and pauses to draw his eyes on me. I immediately recognize him from the picture in Lemrac's utility room –The General. I don't look away. His face is without expression. I can already tell he is as ice cold

as the water in my lungs. The soldiers in the room stand stiff
to attention at the sight of him. A general sense of unease fills
the room like a slow fog. His presence commands attention
and I sense fear within his subordinates in the room. I am
shaken, not by his stature or persona, but by the curious way he
looks at me, with an unsettling familiarity. Other than a long
black handlebar mustache, the general is clean-shaven, even
his head. His uniform is perfectly pressed and decorated with
some metals I recognize and others I do not. The Unimerican
flag is prominently displayed on his left shoulder. It's like the
American Flag except it has black and red stripes and only one
big white star in the blue rectangle. In his hand is a large knife.

I see his mouth moving, but I can't hear the words. My ears
are still damaged from the grenade blast. It doesn't really matter.
I didn't plan on answering him anyway.

He moves closer and I can tell by his expression and body
language that he's speaking much louder. An engraved placard
above his left chest pocket reads TACCA. His name is TACCA,
General Tacca the traitor. I can hear his voice now, but barely.

"Where did you get this," he asks in perfect English,
pressing the point of his knife into the patch on my chest
pocket that reads H. HOYT. With a quick movement, he
presses the knife into my shoulder. I can feel the tip of the
blade; sharp, cold. That knife is familiar. It's the same kind Dad
was issued. I used to love to play with it when I was younger. It
was among the items brought back to us after his passing and it
now rests on the mantle in a wooden cradle I carved.

"Where did you get the shirt, boy," he presses harder.

I say nothing. He twists the knife and presses again. The
razor-sharp point pierces through the wool over shirt and glides
into my flesh, causing excruciating pain. He makes a noise that

sounds like a cross between a question and a grunt and then squints his eyes, watching my response with sadistic arousal. He wants me to be afraid so I lock eyes with him and throw my shoulder forward, thrusting the knife blade deep into my muscle. The pain exits my body as a growling scream, which I direct into his surprised face.

A scout is fearless!

"It was my father's, and he was a real American hero. He would never sell out his country," I say while exhaling, knowing I've probably just said my last words. Tacca's face twists with hate. I spit in his face. If I'm going to die, at least he'll know what I think of him.

I'm surprised I don't feel afraid. I guess a part of me knows there's no point to feeling fear now. I accept whatever happens next. I let it all go: my desire to be with London, to see that everyone I love is safe, to be the man I hoped I would become someday. All I have is right here, right now, and I'm not wasting a second of it in fear. It's the most liberating feeling I've ever had.

I grin at Tacca and laugh out loud and growl at him like an animal, enjoying his flinch of confusion. His hand with the knife hesitates.

I cast a defiant look at the Gi-Nong, as they collectively lean against the back wall, shackled together. The oldest of the warriors gives me a look of silent approval. They understand what I'm doing just as I understood the roar of the mountain lion from across the ravine a few days ago. I am not afraid.

The commander methodically holds up my own machete, still red with the dried blood of the soldier I killed before the grenade exploded. He presses it firmly against my throat. I can feel the sharp blade slice a thin line in the soft skin around my neck. I always keep my machete razor sharp. I stay still. The Gi-Nong slaves watch me, expressionless.

General Tacca leans in close to my ear and growls, "You unlawfully enter my city. You side with my enemies. You free my prisoners and kill my soldiers."

He casts a glance to the line-up of WUG soldiers in the room as if to shame them.

"A boy has done this," he screams with rage.

His voice echoes in the room and is loud even to my damaged ears. He quickly draws the knife away and makes an expression as if he has an idea as to how I might rescue myself from this mess.

"I should slit your throat and leave you in this hole to rot," he continues, "but good talent has become increasingly hard to come by these days." He glares again at the WUG soldiers, whose eyes dart in every direction except towards the enraged General.

"Unchain his hands," he commands to the guard behind me.

A nervous guard fumbles with the keys behind me and the shackles loosen and fall with a crash from my hands to the floor. My forearm aches and as I pull my arms to the front of me I can't help but wince with pain from the fresh wound on my chest.

General Tacca pulls the revolver pistol from the leather holster on his hip and presses the barrel to my forehead. My time has come. He's going to blow my brains out in this dark concrete basement. I hear the soldier behind me shuffle to the side with cautious anticipation.

With a quick flip of his wrist, General Tacca spins the revolver on his index finger so that the grip is facing me. As the

revolver rocks frontwards and backwards on his finger, General
Tacca says in a commanding tone, "Your choice is simple. Swear
allegiance to the WUG and serve under my command as a
WUG mercenary or die by firing squad with the rest of these
swine." With that, he drops the revolver in my lap.

I quickly glance at Falco. His eyes are trained on the general
and me. He's studying what I will do. He's too weak and
battered to fight but I can tell by the look in his eye that he
wants to charge The General with all of his might.

"Pick it up," he commands, motioning toward the Gi-Nong
slaves against the wall. "Pick it up, Mercenary Hoyt. Prove your
loyalty to me and the WUG by killing a slave."

I am not his mercenary. I don't take orders from the
enemy. I want to kill the Gi-Nong, but not like this. Not at
the command of Traitor Tacca. This one act, though, could
buy my freedom. I could kill now and escape later, but my
actions would always haunt me. I'd be trading these chains for a
different kind, equally caging.

But I could see London again, and help Mom and Macy.
I'm no good to them dead. Tacca wants me to kill the people
who killed my father. Is that so bad?

I grip the revolver firmly and aim it at the Gi-Nong slave
directly in front of me. He closes his eyes, with no other
options. Maybe this death is welcome. He's one of the younger
men in the line-up, not much older than me if I had to guess.
Tacca nods in approval. In this moment I feel sorry for the Gi-
Nong.

I can't help but remember the reverence with which my
father spoke of them, often mentioning that he related to the
Gi-Nong more than his fellow soldiers. I can imagine that
in their native jungles, the Gi-Nong are quite an impressive

people. But here, in this cramped, concrete space, they are shackled at both the wrists and the ankles. They look tired, hungry and abused. Like me, they are out of place in this city. Also like me, they are many miles from home. I can tell by the body language that they hate Tacca, too.

I close my left eye to focus my target just above the sighting post on the revolver and spin my torso left to align it with General Tacca's forehead. His eyes widen with surprise but he doesn't move or speak. If I die today, at least I will cut off the head of the snake. Without hesitation, I pull the trigger.

Click. The gun doesn't fire. Click. Click. Click. I pull the trigger as fast as I can three more times. Nothing. I've been tricked. The revolver is empty.

"YOU FOOL," screams General Tacca. "You're just like your father!"

What is he talking about? What does he mean I'm just like my father? The back of his hand crashes across my face and all I see is black for a second. My eyes fill with water and I can feel my nose start to bleed. Pain surges across the muscle, bones and ligaments in my head.

"I commanded your father in the jungles of Asia," he continues. "Hunter Hoyt. One of the best I've ever seen. He could track and kill those Gi-Nong animals in their own jungle like no one else before or after."

I can't believe what I'm hearing. Tacca served in Asia with Dad. What is he talking about? Before I can make sense of it all, he punches me just under the rib cage. Every breath of air exits my body and I'm unable to draw a breath.

"But just like you," he continues, clearly enjoying this. "Your pop started getting soft for the Gi-Nong. He decided their lives mattered more than our mission. Like father, like son.

Now, I'll kill you just as I killed him."

I can't process all that's happening fast enough. Tacca killed Dad? He didn't die in service like the men who brought his things reported to us? His commander murdered him because he did not want to kill innocent people? The Gi-Nong did not kill my Father!

"I'll kill you," I scream, lunging toward General Tacca, falling to the floor with chained ankles. "I'll tear your throat out! Dnoces Tnemdnema!"

The commander looks unimpressed, having no idea what I've just said, but the Gi-Nong warriors cry out with surprise. Almost casually, the commander raises his arm and slams the pommel of my machete into my temple. Lightning streaks through my brain and I struggle to stay conscious.

"Get him out of my sight and take him to the firing line with the rest of this garbage," General Tacca snarls to the guards in the room and motions his hands in a circle around the room. "Make it fast, the drones come in twenty minutes. Meet me at the helicopter in Sector 42."

"Sir, yes, sir," the guards reply in unison.

Everything in the room goes black.

***

A part of my mind knows I'm hallucinating; yet this dream seems so real. I can see the outline of home under the morning mountain mist. I never thought I would see it again. A feeling of excitement rushes through me and I run toward it. Then I see: this is a bad dream. The house isn't as it should be. The flowers are dead in the window boxes. The paint is dingy and peeling. The front gate hangs off its hinges.

"Mom!" I scream. "Macy!"

I burst through the torn screen door and it looks like a

bomb exploded in the middle of the living room. I scream for
Mom and Macy again, but there is no answer.

Now I'm standing on the back porch and I see the meadow
behind our house and it's burned to the ground. The great
valley of pines is gone. My land, my home are decimated.
There's a burnt American flag flying at half-mast on the flagpole.

"Omaaaahaaaa! You let us dowwwwwwnnnnn!
Ommmmaaaaahhaaaaa, wwhhheeeeeeeeeere weeeeerrrreeee
youuuuuuu?" the wind tortures me in Mom's voice.

"Stop it!" I scream. "Stop it! I couldn't help it. They
captured me. I did the best I could!"

A figure stands in the blackened meadow holding its arms
out to me. London! I sprint as hard as I can to reach her, but
my legs are heavy, like I'm running in water. I can't reach her.

"You didn't save me, Omaha," London moans. "You
promised to save me."

She has dark holes for eyes and black tears stream down her
cheeks. I'm being pulled under water. "I tried!" I try to say.

"You saved Nalim, but you didn't save me!"

"No, that's not true," I'm thinking as I drown. "I tried to
save you both!"

The dream turns to reality as I gain consciousness and
realize I really am drowning in cold blackness. I struggle weakly
against the hand holding me under. I think this is it, the end,
because my body is out of air and there's nothing I can do but
drift away. I give up struggling and start to fade away.

My head is flung backward out of the water and I'm
coughing and sputtering, to get the water out of my lungs. They
barely give me time to recover when a gun barrel presses against
the back of my head. They have to drag me up two flights of
stairs because I am too weak to walk and I don't bother trying.

Let them shoot me here and save me the trouble. I'm ready to die.

The sun blinds me for a moment when we exit the building into the square, just steps from London's rosebush planter. I check the angle of light and calculate that it's late afternoon. Hours have passed since my friends escaped (I will believe they escaped; the alternative is unacceptable). I feel a deep ache of regret that I'm not with them, but I will wait for them in the great meadow beyond the skies. I wonder if Dad and Grandpa will be waiting for me there. I guess I'll find out soon.

I'm marched to the concrete wall, where the firing squads are still at work. They dump me near the end, the fifth prisoner in line to be executed. Falco is next to me, number six, slumped in a pile on the ground. He is either already dead or unconscious, I can't tell. I say his name but there is no response. I want to help him but I can barely stand myself, still trying to catch my breath and dizzy from what feels like could be a concussion.

By the looks of it, we are the last of the prisoners scheduled for execution. The holding pen is now empty. Only seven soldiers remain and one almost-full dump truck idles nearby, waiting for us to die so we can be dumped with the rest of the bodies by the river. The truck makes a loud beeping noise as it backs up to the gate a few feet away, and I register the fact that my hearing is just about back to normal – not that it will matter when they shoot me. The driver doesn't even bother to turn off the engine. I suppose the wait won't be that long. The four Gi-Nong slaves wait nearby to pitch our dead bodies into the back. Their eyes are trained on me. Under other circumstances, we could be allies in this moment. They are not my enemy. Not in this place. They did not kill my father. We are both enemies of the WUG.

The concrete wall behind me is red with blood and smeared with flecks of flesh and bone and hair. I hear the sound of bullets falling into chambers as the soldiers load our deaths into their guns. The spring breeze is pleasant and the sun feels good on my wet body. I only wish I could have had one last day in the meadow with London and that I could tell Nalim how grateful I am for everything she's done for me.

One of the remaining WUG guards barks an order and I close my eyes to accept my fate. A piercing sound echoes through the square, but it's not gunshots. I know that sound. I open my eyes and smile at the eagle circling in the sky above me. I am still smiling as I turn my head to follow its flight.

Suddenly, a shot is fired. The broken fingered man is first in the line-up and drops to the ground and blood sprays the wall. The woman with the shaved head is beside me, shaking with fear, her teeth chattering uncontrollably. I want to comfort her, but I have no words. I tap her shoulder and point to the sky so she, too, can see the eagle that comforts me.

We watch the eagle soar in the great blue freedom of the air and I thank it for coming in this final moment of my life to remind me what's important. For the first time in this long journey I feel my father and grandfather watching over me, and it's as comforting as a warm blanket on a cold night. Another screech blesses the bright sky. A Gi-Nong slave points. They are also watching the eagle. A WUG soldier takes aim at the eagle, shoots and misses. The eagle quickly shifts in flight. The other soldiers laugh roughly and say something to him. My eyes find the old Gi-Nong warrior. He is staring at me, expressionless, curious.

Another shot, and this time it's the prisoner with the black hood whose brains are splattered against the wall.

My world goes silent as I watch the eagle's shadow move quietly along the cobblestones of the square. A third shot, this time again at the eagle. It draws gunfire as it circles closer, taunting the WUG soldiers.

With each circling pass, the eagle's shadow moves closer to me until finally it crosses right through me. As I watch it slice across my legs and feet I notice a charred chunk of wood on the ground. I stoop down and pick it up.

I am the son of H. Hoyt, an Eagle among men.

I turn and stretch out my shackled hands and write a big, bold set of eagle wings with a number 1 and 2 in each wing. Dad and Grandpa will understand. It stands out boldly on the bloodstained concrete wall. It is my last testament before I turn to charge the death-dealers. I will die fighting not waiting.

Another shot and the woman next to me is dead. Her blood sprays my right side. I will be next. I get ready to lunge. I probably won't make it far in these shackles, but at least I'll go down trying.

Suddenly, the Gi-Nong warriors move as one. They raise their shackles and charge the WUG firing line in complete silence, but once they have their chains wrapped around the soldiers' necks, they yell an unmistakable war cry. I stoop down and grab a big chunk of concrete and hurl it at a WUG soldier who is taking aim at the Gi-Nong. It smashes into the side of his face and knocks him sideways. Within seconds, I am on top of him and one more blow with the piece of rubble is all it takes. I grab his gun and shoot another soldier in the back just as he fires his gun. A young Gi-Nong warrior leaps through the air and wraps his shackle chain around the WUG guard's throat, dragging him to the ground. He slices the soldier's jugular with my machete, which the guard was wearing on his belt. I kill the last retreating WUG soldier with a single shot to the head. It took less than a minute and the battle is over.

The Gi-Nong warriors chant in their strange language as they kill three wounded WUG soldiers. They find the keys and unlock their shackles. The young Gi-Nong warrior and the old one walk over to me. I recognize him as the warrior I took aim at earlier in the concrete room. I'm uncertain whether we are now allies or enemies. I grip the gun firmly. The young warrior tosses the keys to my shackles through the air, which I catch with my good hand.

We are allies.

The old warrior approaches slowly and draws in close to my face. The deep wrinkles along his mouth and eyes tell the story of a hard life. I wonder if the long scar across his forehead was caused by man or beast. He slants his head to the side as his eyes intently study my face. He traces the faded eagle wings across my eyes with his finger then grabs me by the mouth and forcefully turns my head to one side and then the other. I suspect he's looking at the remnants of the viper and lion track symbols on my cheeks. Up close, I can see a small white bone pierces through the center of his nose. A tattoo of black and yellow dots adorns his face. Gaping holes in his ear lobes show where he once had wood dowels dangling with feathers, just like Dad described to me. He motions to the younger warrior.

He resembles the old man and must be his son. His face is also tattooed. Solid black covers his lower lip down to his neck and a long yellow stripe stretching from the tip of his nose to the hairline above his forehead. A thin white sliver of bone connects a hole on the top and bottom of each ear, where the teeth of some small animal dangle from a piece of plant fiber cordage around his neck.

"Where you see that?" the young warrior asks in very broken English while pointing to the charred eagle wing symbol on the concrete wall.

"It is a symbol of my family," I reply. "My father and grandfather had it tattooed here." I point to my forearm. "It represents an oath that we have taken."

The old man looks me up and down. Then he yanks up his sleeve to reveal a crude tattoo of the eagle symbol on his forearm.

I blink several times to make sure I'm not seeing things. How can this be? How can this Gi-Nong warrior have the same tattoo as my father and grandfather?

Before I can speak, the young warrior pulls up the tattered sleeve of the work camp uniform and points to the same tattoo on his own arm and says, "Eagle man save my father's life."

CHAPTER FOURTEEN

I'm alive! Saved by the Gi-Nong, and I can hardly process what's happening. The dump truck pulls up with a screech, driven by a fifth Gi-Nong who I haven't seen yet. The young warrior motions to get in.

"I can't leave Falco," I say, pointing to his lifeless body still at the same spot in the firing line.

They help me drag Nalim's father into the truck and then they pile in with us – seven of us crammed into a dump truck full of dead bodies racing through the destroyed city of Philadelphia, racing to get out as fast as possible because we can hear the buzz of drones heading our way. The bombing is about to begin.

I should be worried about surviving; I should be grateful that I wasn't shot. But what I need now, more than anything, is to understand what has happened. The Gi-Nong wear my family's symbol. They saved my life. While one of the warriors drives, the old man's son tells me, in very crude English, how a man was sent to kill the Gi-Nong people, but instead helped them by betraying his own people. They gave this man a sacred weapon of the Gi-Nong people.

With a sense of unreality, I reach deep into the cargo pocket of my pants and pull out the slingshot Dad gave me before he died. The young warrior's eyes widen in disbelief. He says something fast in a Gi-Nong language to the others. They pass around my slingshot with wonder in their eyes.

All of Dad's and my conversations about the Gi-Nong start to make sense to me now – his respect for them and their culture. The young warrior finishes the story.

"My father is captured, but eagle man sneak him out and my father run away. This man come back many months later, he help us many times, but then he is seen by his own soldiers and they shoot him. So we put his mark on our arms to remember eagle friend of the Gi-Nong."

Dnoces Tnemdnema. Dad risked everything for what he felt was right. I point to the eagle tattoo on the warrior's forearm.

"He was my father. He was fearless."

***

Before anyone can respond, an explosion shakes the ground like an earthquake, sending the truck a few feet into the air. Skyscrapers sway back and forth alarmingly and I instinctively cover my head – not that it will help if they come crumbling down on us. The drones are not quite above us, but they are getting closer. Bombs are gliding down all over the city. If it's going to be anything like the destruction of the other big cities, then it will be over in minutes. Burning ash is already raining down on the square. In the distance I see a helicopter, ahead of the bombers, leaving the city. It must be General Tacca. I wonder for a moment if he has any idea I'm not dead yet.

Miraculously, the road is still clear and the truck barrels south, away from the center where the bombs are falling. The sky behind us darkens with a plume of smoke that reaches the heavens. Rocks and debris clatter onto the windshield. A wall of heat overtakes us and I tuck my head down to protect my eyes. A chunk of charred concrete smashes through the canvas roof and crashes into the pile of bodies on the opposite side of the truck bed. Another tears through at a diagonal, splintering one of the wooden support rails.

The WUG ground forces have already evacuated. The streets are completely deserted. As the truck gets clear of the immediate destruction and we're rolling along at a good pace I turn my attention to Falco. I check his pulse, relieved to find he has one.

While he's unconscious I tear away his pant leg from around the disjointed knee. When I was a boy, Dad made me help him with a goat that had dislocated its leg. Using my own leg as leverage I try to work and twist the knee back into socket. The pain must be incredible because he comes to screaming, and then slips back into unconsciousness just as quickly. Before too long, I finally feel the knee slip back into joint. I use a chunk of the splintered wooden support rail and tie on a makeshift splint using two boards and strips of fabric from his pant leg. Just as I finish, the truck screeches to a halt.

The young warrior turns his head toward the back.

"You go here!" he yells.

"Come with me!" I say, throwing Falco's arm around my neck and pulling him from the truck.

"We cannot," he says, and I remember the hostages the WUG keeps to ensure their obedience.

"What's your name," I ask before he leaves.

"Maiga," he responds. "I am called Maiga."

"I am Omaha," I respond.

He hands me my machete, which I didn't even know he had, and he holds up his eagle tattoo like some kind of farewell.

"Good luck son of Eagle man," he says.

I can't think of a proper way to say goodbye, so I say, "Dnoces Tnemdnema." He nods in agreement and the truck takes off. The Gi-Nong are my friends and I wish we were not parting ways. There's so much left unsaid, but they have to go find their loved ones. I do too.

Falco's weight on my wounded body is almost unbearable. I have to drag him, and we're moving too slow. We're barely outside the city limits and the ground is shaking from the massive explosions that are too close for comfort. I adjust my buckskin scarf so that it covers my nose and mouth as some protection from the toxic ash that's covering us steadily. Even though it's late afternoon, the smoke and ash block the sun and turn the sky an eerie green hue.

This is what the apocalypse looks like, I think to myself.

I need to get my bearings. I no longer have my map, but I can see the river so I know we're not far from where Nalim and I first entered the city. I drag Falco painfully over to the embankment and recognize the concrete slope that leads down from the tunnels to the cedar swamp where the boats are hidden. The dead refugees are still piled up in the same place where we left them – how long ago was that? Two days? It seems unreal.

I take my chances that the guards have abandoned the watchtowers and the patrol boats are gone. It's exhausting and painful work, but I manage to drag Falco down the concrete

embankment and into the cedar swamp to the boats. They
are all still there, completely undisturbed. That worries me,
because I'd assumed Nalim would use the boats to escape. Are
they still in the tunnels? The thought is too terrible to consider.
I have to believe they are safe.

Small pieces of rubble and burning embers occasionally tear
through the soft cedar canopy, but in general, this is a pretty
decent place to regroup and refuel. It will be dark soon, and I
have no light. I focus on a plan for the night.

Falco is still out cold, so I take a few minutes to construct
a small shelter. I flip one of the boats on its side and prop it up
with a fallen tree. I insulate the ground underneath with cedar
boughs and roll Falco inside. It's just large enough for the both
of us and will protect us through the night from falling debris
and rain if it comes.

I spend the next hour or so hunting and gathering, which
is challenging with the ground covered in ash. I tap a few river
birch trees for drinkable sap – not as delicious as maple, but it
will keep us hydrated. I almost fill a 2-liter bottle I find at the
river's edge. While it fills, I carve munti from a stand of willow
saplings. The wildlife have all fled the bombing and I doubt
I'll find anything to hunt, but then I'm surprised to hear the
coo of pigeons right over my head. I take down two who were
sheltering in the cedars from the burning ash. Digging around
near the river, I find a few bull thistle roots and cattail rhizomes
– probably not too clean with all of the trash from the city,
but I'll eat them anyway. I have to have strength to make the
journey back.

I build a large tinder bundle from some dry shredded
cedar bark and mix it with fluffy cattail seeds. I could make a
primitive bow-and-drill fire set to create the ember I need to

ignite the tinder bundle, but I decide to conserve my energy and wait for a smoldering piece of ash to fall from the sky. Within a few minutes I catch a nice ember and blow my tinder bundle into flame with no problem at all. I never thought I would see the day when the ember I needed to start a survival fire would literally fall from the heavens.

While the pigeons and roots are roasting I tend to Falco. Though not totally conscious, he is able to occasionally swallow some birch water when I pour it in his mouth. I don't know how long he's been without food or water but I can tell by how parched his lips and mouth are that he needs to be hydrated. He may have internal injuries, but all I can try to fix is his knee, which must have taken a beating when I dragged him down here. The splint has loosened and the swelling has gone down a bit since I tied it on in the truck several hours ago, which is actually a good sign. I reset the splint and make sure to bind it nice and tight.

In the last bit of fading green light I make a funnel-style fish trap from some netting I find hung up on an old log, and I make some hoops from a few small mulberry saplings. I bait the trap with the pigeon entrails and weight it with a rock at the edge of the river. Hopefully, breakfast will be waiting for us tomorrow morning.

When I get back to the shelter Falco's breathing is labored. I'm able to stir him just enough to take a few more gulps of birch water, but I'm still not able to make sense of his delirious ramblings. He falls back into a deep sleep. I lean one of the other boats against our roof. It will block the firelight and keep anyone from seeing us from the road above, and it will also act as a fire reflector. The nights are still chilly and I want to keep Falco warm. I gather a big pile of driftwood from the edge of the river to burn throughout the night.

I wait for the food to cook and my mind is working overtime, making plans and reviewing my memory of maps and routes home. I keep replaying the moment when London and I were together in the square before she escaped into the manhole. She was so alive, so beautiful and clever, as she always has been. And Rake calling me "Reuben." The memory makes me smile. But he couldn't walk on his own. How could they possibly have gotten him through the tunnels? And Nalim only had two gas masks for the three of them. How many bullets did she have left? Supplies? She did have my bug out bag. Worries swirl around in my head and it's absolute torture.

I coat my chapped lips with some of the melted pigeon fat and feast on the cooked meat and roots. The crispy pigeon skin is absolutely delicious. The roasted cattail roots are sweet and gooey. I feel refreshed with energy as the protein, carbohydrates and starch work their way through my digestive system. I'm so grateful again to the Boy Scouts and Dad and Grandpa for teaching me so many things, like first aid and how to feed myself in the wild. And maybe most of all for giving me the confidence to know I can take care of myself.

Even though I could eat twice as much as I have, I prudently save a few roots and one pigeon for Falco. He will need it to give his broken and battered body a boost, and he'll need all the strength he can get to travel with me tomorrow morning. I want to get on the road toward home as soon as possible and we need to get away from Philadelphia as fast as we can.

I doze on and off, waking when Falco struggles with delirious nightmares and coughing spells. He yells for Nalim and Lemrac and thrashes around. I take these moments to stoke the fire with more driftwood and give him sips of birch water. Despite the cool, damp air, our shelter is quite comfortable and the fire-warmed metal boats radiate a nice steady heat. The explosions ended hours ago. I know Philadelphia is completely flattened. There are no sirens or rumbles from WUG trucks, and no staccato sounds of firing lines. The General has moved on to the next great city, I think bleakly. Will they ever stop? Is this how it will be from now on? Will we ever go back to being the America we once were?

When I awake, at least six inches of ash covers the ground outside of the shelter. I daydream for a second that Grandpa and I are out on one of our winter elk hunts and we're just waking up to track them in the fresh morning powder. A deep cough from Falco brings me back to reality. As I turn in his direction, I'm surprised to see his eyes are open.

"Where are we?" he mutters weakly. "And who are you?"

"I'm Omaha, a friend of Nalim," I reply. His eyes go wide with wonder at hearing his daughter's name. "We made it out of the city, by your boats."

"Where is Nalim? Where is Lemrac?" His voice shakes as he fights back a deep, congested cough.

"Lemrac is dead," I tell him. "He died saving Nalim. I don't know where Nalim is. The last time I saw her was in the tunnels heading out of Philadelphia with two of my friends. I was captured by the WUG and put into the interrogation room with you. I don't know if they made it."

"That was you in the tunnels when she came to see me?" He coughs violently and it sounds like his chest is filled with syrup. He strains hard to breathe and I watch as a thin line of blood seeps from one of his nostrils. My hope of saving Falco fades.

"Yes," I say gently. "Would you like some food?" I tear off

some cold pigeon meat and offer it to him.

"I'm in no condition to eat, son. I'm dying," he calmly whispers. "Tell me how you met my daughter."

Falco closes his eyes as I tell him the story of everything that happened since I first rescued Nalim from the WUG truck. I tell him how Nalim saved my life and how she's one of the bravest people I've ever met and how it killed her to leave him behind in the gallows. I tell him how much she loves him, even though he already knows this. A tear slides down his cheek.

"You risked your life for my daughter. Now you've risked your life for me." It's quiet for a minute except for the painful sound of Falco breathing.

"I'm a Boy Scout," I say, and then I feel embarrassed. That must have sounded random to him but he opens his eyes wider.

"I see," he says. "And also an enemy of the WUG."

I grin at him. He grins back and then winces with pain.

"So Boy Scout, what do you want?" he asks, sounding a lot like Nalim right then.

What do I want? What do I want?! I want to see my friends and family again. I want to live happily on a farm somewhere with my own family one day. But none of that is enough anymore.

"I want the world to be like it was before the WUG," I tell him, putting into words for the first time what I've been feeling during this long, painful journey. "I want the people of this country to be free. I want the pain and hurt and sadness to go away. I want America back. I want to see my friends and family again. And, I want to kill Tacca."

Falco grasps my wrists with a surprisingly strong grip.

"Omaha," he says, "then you must fight for her!"

I assume by her that he means America but I can't tell for

sure. He's still a little delirious.

Falco breaks into another coughing spell, the worst yet. I can see blood in his mouth now. I hold his shoulder to keep him from falling over.

"You can't save me, son," he says in a raspy whisper. "And it's not your fault. Promise me something. Take care of my Nalim when you find her."

Before I can tell him I will, he pulls me in close. "I was almost dead in the gallows when I heard an eagle cry out. Can you believe that? An eagle flying over Philadelphia—the chaos and gunfire." He takes a few seconds to catch his breath. "This eagle, the symbol of our nation's freedom, gave me hope," whispers Falco. "You are the hope, son. I know it."

When he calls me "son" I feel a strange knowing in my gut. That eagle – it was Dad. I feel it in my gut. He was reaching out to me, helping me. I'm so moved by this understanding that I feel tears in my eyes.

Falco is fumbling at his neck with stiff fingers. He breaks off a leather necklace at the end of which dangles a bronzed eagle talon. He presses it into my hands.

"Will you finish what I cannot? Will you take my burden, take this key, and free us? Will you?"

I don't understand what he means. What is his burden and how can this talon be a key? A key to what? Thinking he's delirious, I tell him, "I will." I tie the necklace around my neck.

He watches me, his eyes bright. I don't want him to die. Maybe he's just weak. I move the food where he can reach it and say, "You have to get strong now so I can take you to Nalim." He doesn't answer, but I'm determined to keep him alive. I climb out from under the boat shelter and cut down an ironwood sapling to make a walking crutch for Falco.

"Ironwood is very strong and will easily hold your weight," I say as I cut a section from the sapling with a wide Y fork at one end that he can place under his arm to brace himself. "Look, we'll pad it with dried grass and I'll just tie it on with some of the leftover netting from the fish trap I made last night," I say.

He isn't answering. I duck back under the boats and find him slumped over sideways, laying peacefully across the bed of cedar bows. He's gone.

"No!" I scream into the cedar canopy above.

I grab Falco's shoulder and shake him. "Don't die on me. Don't you die on me! Not now. Not this close."

There is no response. He's really gone. I sit beside his battered body and cry, not for Falco or myself but for Nalim.

I've seen so much death in the last week, and killed more people than I can count, but losing Falco feels…it feels like losing Dad. They seemed so similar; and they were both warriors, giving up their lives for what they believed in.

I grasp the eagle talon in my left fist and feel it shift slightly. I take it off so I can look at it more closely. It feels almost like a locket and examining it closely I see a cleverly hidden seam. I slide one side away from the other against the seam and it opens a crack. I shake it to see if anything is inside and a small green and gold, metallic square slides out. It's some type of small computer drive. Is this the burden Falco was talking about? Whatever is on this, I know it's dangerous, and I know it has something to do with taking down the WUG. I carefully put it back in the talon and close it securely. I tie the bronze talon pendant necklace back around my neck.

Before I bury Falco, I eat a few bites of the cooked pigeon. I know he'd understand. I need the energy. There is a spot beneath the cedar canopy where sunlight strikes the thick, moss-blanketed ground. It is a good resting place for this battered warrior who kept up the fight until his very last breath. I fashion a cross from two pieces of driftwood and lash it to a nearby tree with scrap wire. I place my machete in the remaining hot coals of the fire until the blade is red hot and burn FALCO on the cross beneath the eagle symbol. This symbol is about more than just our family now. It is a symbol of hope and freedom. America is worth fighting for and dying for. Dnoces Tnemdnema.

I kneel and place my hand on the center of Falco's grave. The fresh dirt is cool and moist.

"I'll take care of her," I whisper. "I promise."

Then, I close my eyes and say the only prayer I know.

If he is lost, guide his steps.
If he is shaken, steady his sights.
If he is alone, comfort his soul.
Finally, if he is worthy, take him home.

Chapter Fifteen

I'm all alone as I start my journey home. My whole life I've always preferred to be alone, but as I limp along down the riverbank, I realize I feel lonely. The woods are not enough for me now. I wish Nalim were walking beside me, telling me why it's important to fight the WUG. I wish I could hear London tell me how she and Rake managed to stay alive when the WUG quarantined Philadelphia. I wish I could hear Rake call me "Reuben," and I really wish I could thank him for helping London. I even wish Lemrac, who I didn't know that well, was along on the journey. I miss the brave comrade. Heck, I even wish the Gi-Nong warriors were here. I have a thousand more questions to ask them about Dad.

After everything I've been through, I feel emotionally numb. I have no tears, no anger. I have – realizing this with no emotion – no hope anymore. When I think about it honestly, I don't believe my friends made it out of the tunnels alive. The soldiers knew they were there; Rake was crippled; London was so weak; there were only two gas masks for the three of them. I feel bleak. The only thing keeping me putting one foot in front of the other is the thought of Mom and Macy waiting for me.

After two hours of steady, but slow, walking, I take a break. I sweep the thick layer of ash off a boulder and specs of embedded quartz glitter on the surface in the sun. That's when I notice that the sky is clear again, pretending to be a normal day even though the world will never be normal for me again. I methodically inventory my resources, laying each item on the coarse gray surface. I wish I had my bug out bag. The items I do have include my machete, slingshot, 12 munti, a plastic bag that holds most of a cooked pigeon, a handful of cooked roots, a 2-liter plastic bottle with about two cups of birch sap, plus the clothes on my back and an oven with a catfish slow-baking.

Before I left the cedar grove, I'd checked the fish trap and found two decent-sized fish waiting for me – a catfish and a type I didn't recognize. I kept the catfish and let the other one go. Rather than stoking the dying fire and wait for the fish to cook, I've been cooking it while I hike. I fastened a wooden handle to an old tin coffee can I found half buried in river mud. After washing out the can in the river, I filled the bottom with hot coals from the fire and then lay great burdock leaves on top of the coals. I cleaned the fish and stuffed it with two handfuls of wild ramps I found poking out through the ash in the woods. Then I placed the fish on top of the leaves, layered on more hot coals and picked the portable oven up by the handle. The fish is still cooking, but I decide to wait until later to eat it. But I add the metal can to my gear inventory. I can use it to boil and purify water later if necessary.

I also take a mental inventory of my body. My lion-clawed calf still makes travel difficult, but so far neither my leg nor my arm – still sore, but healing – seem to be infected, thank God. My shoulder aches from General Tacca's knife, but it was a clean cut. The gash on my head is very tender and hot. I'll have to keep an eye on it, maybe boil some water to clean it out later. My ribs are bruised and my lungs hurt sharply when I draw a big breath. All in all, I'm grateful to be alive and mobile, but I can't ignore my fatigue. I'm impatient to get home, but I can't push myself too hard or I could make things worse. "Not a river or a fool," I mutter out loud. I wish Grandpa were here to offer me more words of wisdom.

I start walking again through the devastated landscape. Random fires from last night's toxic ash storm burn in patches beside the river. I see no other tracks in the ash, which completely blanket the ground. It seems the animals have all taken cover. I don't blame them, but that will make it hard for me to find dinner. About seven miles away from the city I finally spot a rabbit track leading to the river. I silently load my slingshot, but there is no sign of it. I keep walking.

With no one to distract me from my thoughts, my mind spins with questions. How can Mom, Macy and I prepare for the inevitable appearance of the WUG on our farm? It's only a matter of time. Before this journey, I thought we could hide and wait them out, but I know now that's naïve. They won't go away. Our little bunker nestled in the Rosa Rugosa patch can't be our long-term strategy. We can't hide there forever.

The bronze talon capsule is cool against my chest. What information does the shiny drive contain? Falco suggested that the talon holds the key to a future free from WUG rule, but it seems grandiose to think I'll be the one to make it happen. What did Falco mean about carrying the burden and delivering it?

The one piece of news I'm eager to tell Mom and Macy is how Dad really died. They'll be glad to know that he was true to himself to the end, and that his actions in the jungles of South Asia ended up saving me from death in Philadelphia. What a story I have to tell when I get home.

Dad lives in me through his teachings and speaks to me through my memories of our times together. I will tell Mom how he watched over me when I fought the big cat, and how he guided my eyes with the eagle's shadow to the charcoal that I used to scribe our symbol on the wall that ultimately led the Gi-Nong to free me. Just as Grandpa always used to say, the spirits of our ancestors are always with us. They whisper to us in the winds, calm us with the glow of a crackling fire, and lead us on wings of eagles. Goosebumps climb up my spine as I think about Dad and Grandpa and our ancestors leading and guiding me on this journey to and from Philadelphia.

If they are guiding me, then they may also be guiding those I love. I pray that London, Nalim and Rake are still alive.

Suddenly, I hear a loud screech far above the forest canopy. My heart soars with hope. Even though I can't see it, I know the eagle flies high above me. I want so badly to believe it's a sign that my friends are still alive.

***

Hours later, my stomach reminds me that it's time to refuel. The scent of baked catfish in my mobile oven makes my mouth water. A large, fallen walnut tree near the edge of the Delaware River is the perfect spot to stop. I dump the contents of my tin can onto the tree and brush away the still-hot coals with my machete. I gently peel away the juice-soaked burdock leaves to reveal a perfectly cooked, piping-hot catfish.

"Ha!" I say aloud. "It worked!"

I stab bits of the flaky flesh with a small skewer I carved from one of the walnut branches. The wild ramps give the meat a sweet onion flavor. It is delicious and would be perfect with a basket of Mom's dandelion fritters, but I'll have to wait until I get home for those. The catfish is reduced to bones in a matter of minutes and the caramelized leeks make a perfect dessert. Before I hit the trail again I wrap two of the remaining hot coals in a bundle of dried cattail seed heads I find along the river's edge. The coals will smolder inside the tightly packed cattail cobs and will make starting a fire later this evening much easier. My tin-can oven makes the perfect carrying container for this smoldering bundle. I also pluck a handful of walnuts that still hang on the branches from last fall. The nuts inside are probably spoiled, but I may be able to use them as bait for a squirrel snare later on.

With food in my belly and a burst of energy, I decide to leave the river and start cutting west through the woods. The game trail I'm following leads directly through a dense cluster of black spruce trees. Grandpa got me hooked on spruce gum when I was a little boy and I've preferred it over the store-bought stuff ever since. As I move from tree to tree, my mouth waters with anticipation. When a black spruce is injured, the spruce sap will ooze from the wound and harden to form amber-colored clusters. I snap off a small, hard ball of sap from a nearby tree and pop it in my mouth. The heat of my mouth softens the hard nodule in just a few seconds. Soon, I'm chewing away on one of my favorite forest candies. It's not sweet like Wrigley's, but it has a refreshing pine flavor that makes me feel alive. I love chewing spruce gum on a hike.

Normally, I would graze on wild edible plants during a hike like this, but since everything is covered in ash I shred off strips of cooked pigeon instead. It's cold, but still very good. I'm on constant lookout for more wild game, but haven't seen much besides a few small songbirds and I'm not that desperate yet. I wonder how far west the ash of Philadelphia has blown. The soft gray blanket is still playing tricks on my mind and makes it seem colder than it really is. The sky is clear now and the sun is bright orange and setting fast. I will soon have to think about shelter for tonight, but my goal is to make it to the small grass lean-to that Nalim built in the valley the night I killed the big cat. I think about her for a moment, and how she would tease me for "playing Boy Scouts" now.

Before long I make it to the stream that Nalim and I followed to the Delaware River from her lean-to. I managed to make almost a full day's trek from the city, which is good news. The bad news is the ground is still covered in ash and I haven't seen signs of human travel. I'm slowly resigning myself to the truth that they are gone.

Then something occurs to me: how long was I unconscious before the water torture started? I remember London and Rake making it into the manhole and then the grenade went off, and I assumed I came to a short time later. But what if it was a whole day later? They could be days ahead of me if that's true!

I quickly talk myself back down. The odds were still largely against them getting out. WUG soldiers saw them go into the hole and would certainly have followed or thrown grenades down. Even if they made it through the tunnels, they could have been shot by guards while making their way out. The odds of them making it out alive are minuscule and I need to accept it once and for all. The guilt of being alive when they are dead grows with every step I take away from Philadelphia. As the deep orange sun sinks into the horizon ahead of me, I'm hit with real grief.

It comes in waves, like nausea. It tears at my heart and my stomach, and I feel trapped, crippled with a claustrophobic feeling. My mind is too broken to hold the line of defense against survival's greatest enemy. Panic is taking over. I'm alone, everyone I love is dead. I can't protect anyone. I try to take calming breaths but I can't. I imagine home where Mom and Macy are waiting for me, but it's not enough. I desperately search the sky above for the eagle's comfort, but it, too, has abandoned me. I'm hyperventilating. My body starts to tremble uncontrollably and I crash, helpless, into the ash–covered, sandy dirt below.

I'm in no condition to build a suitable shelter for the night. The sun is setting fast and I know I'm not far from Nalim's grass lean-to, but I can't push myself any farther. I have lost my will to go on. I won't mind if this ashy valley becomes my final resting place. All I want to do is give up. I've had enough: my body is battered; my mind is weary; my heart is broken; my faith is lost. I don't try to hold back the tears or the pain. I realize I'm not fearless. But it's not death I fear; it's life. I'm afraid of living without her. I can't imagine how I can do it without the girl who changed my life with just one look. Few people ever meet that one person who is their light in a dark world. She was my light. She was my hope for a better tomorrow. With her by my side, I could dream. No matter how bad things got, she was all I needed. Any happiness from this moment forward will be because something reminds me of her and even then it will be followed by sadness.

"I can't go on," I cry to whatever or whoever will listen.

The silence of my loneliness is deafening. Grandpa told me when I was a very young boy, "Omaha, when you're in nature you're never alone."

I feel so alone. It's unbearable. So I close my eyes and really listen, trying desperately to center myself and regain control of my wildly out-of-control thoughts. I hear the babbling stream beside me. It reminds me of the brook at home that leads to the pond. I remember Mom's last words to me, "I can't lose you, too." A squirrel barks at me from a nearby branch. I acknowledge its words of encouragement with a quick glance up. A beetle tunnels through the rotting tree just a few feet away and reminds me that even the smallest creature can make a difference in a big world. I recognize the smells of the forest and I open my eyes to see the orange and pink clouds of the world turning to night. Nature begins to revive me, and then – like a miracle - a shadow glides across the ground in front of me. The eagle still soars above. I have not been deserted. I am not alone. I cannot give up. I must keep going. Like Nalim said, this is bigger than me. I'm beginning finally to understand.

Nalim continued to fight the WUG even though she had nothing left to fight for. She understood. My father fought for something bigger than himself, even though it meant never seeing his family again. He understood. Lemrac, the great warrior, battled impossible odds to save Nalim and me. He understood. Falco gave his life protecting the hope of a new world. He understood. If I give up now, I will let everyone down who ever believed in me and that is the worst failure of all. I finally understand what it means to be FEARLESS. It is the refusal to give up hope regardless of the circumstances.

I force myself onto my knees. I welcome the stabbing pain in my arm, calf and shoulder. It reminds me that I am still alive. A cool breeze blows across my face and its soothing embrace calms me.

I sniff. There is something familiar in that breeze. I can't name it, but it makes me feel warm and good inside.

Campfire smoke. I am smelling a campfire!

"My friends!" I shout, springing to my feet. "My love!"

I run along the stream and around the tight bend ahead. The bright setting sun meets me at the corner. The sky is painted with a palette of reds, oranges and yellows. I plunge into the tall wall of reed grass, beyond which is Nalim's lean-to. I squint to see, but the brilliant sun blinds me. I feel trapped in one of those dreams where you can't see or get to what you want and need more desperately than anything.

"Hello?" I call toward the shelter. I call again, louder, "Hello?"

Silhouettes appear from behind the shelter.

"Omaha!" she shrieks.

Though I can't see her, every fragment of my being knows who is calling my name.

"Omaha!" she screams again.

The one girl who I can't survive without is alive. As her silhouette approaches I collapse into the reeds. The eagle screeches high above in celebration. She is alive! My prayers are answered.

I was lost.
I was shaken.
I was never alone.
Finally, I am home.

Also by Creek Stewart:

<u>Nonfiction</u>
Build the Perfect Bug Out Bag
Build the Perfect Bug Out Vehicle
Build the Perfect Bug Out Survival Skills
The Unofficial Hunger Games Wilderness Survival Guide
365 Essential Survival Skills

<u>Fiction</u>
STUCK: A Survival Short Story

Subscribe for updates at http://www.creekstewart.com

Please share this book with your friends on social media -
#rugosa

CPSIA information can be obtained
at www.ICGtesting.com
Printed in the USA
LVOW12s0324280617
539549LV00002B/8/P